The Long Journey
and Other Stories

Jerry Mills, D.M.D.

© 2011 Jerry Mills D.M.D.
All Rights Reserved.

No part of this publication may be reproduced, stored in a retrieval system, or transmitted, in any form or by any means, electronic, mechanical, photocopying, recording, or otherwise, without the written permission of the author.

First published by Dog Ear Publishing
4010 W. 86th Street, Ste H
Indianapolis, IN 46268
www.dogearpublishing.net

ISBN: 978-145750-120-3

This book is printed on acid-free paper.

Printed in the United States of America

This book is dedicated
to my wife
Alyce (O'Riley, O'Gregory) Mills.

About the cover

This simple sketch is over 100 years old. It hung in the farm house I was raised in as a small boy. The artist was a relative on the Jackson side of my family tree. The original sketch now hangs in the cabin where I live.

My grandmother tried to explain the meaning of the sketch to me when I was eight years old, but it was way over my head. Now that I have entered the final chapter of my long journey, I look at the sketch a lot differently than I did when my grandmom talked to me about it so long ago.

The old man is not only old but very wise. The sweet, mellow smell from his pipe is now an integral part of him. The fragrance of Spring completely surrounds the young girl. As she tells him about his upcoming long journey, you can see the slight smile on his face. He knows his next journey will be soon and very short. I suspect that he will give her very little advice. He knows that unraveling the mysteries and finding your own answers are what make our long journeys worthwhile.

Poppy

About the stories

You may find some of them are sad, some funny, and some a little mysterious. However, I hope they rekindle and stir emotions you have hidden deep inside you—for a very long time.

Contents

The Long Journey 1
The Big Operation..6
"We'll Leave The Light On For You"..11
Going Home Is A Little Dusty Now 14
Understanding Special Pain 16
Spit In the Devil's Eye 18
The Ritual 20
Richard's Vacation 23
Memories of the Ol' Poppy Pitch 25
The Cleansing 27
Boundary Waters 31
The Duck Supper 36
Alex..38
The Hobo Who Wasn't..40
Squirt...43
Papa's Cold North Wind...47
Dreams of Home 53
Dab 56
The Shoe Shine Boy 61
The Daisy Church 64
The Call Home..67
The Circle 69
Miracles...72
Box of Dreams 75
Boo-Ray, Sweet Thing and Sidney 81
Three Pats 87

The Long Journey

As the old man stepped up on the back porch of the old funeral home and read the name on the door—Brown Funeral Home, Clinton, Kentucky—he wondered how many kinfolks, friends and neighbors had gone through these doors in the course of time. Some, he thought, carried sadness, while others a feeling of relief.

He had come to visit an old friend whose long journey had ended. The old man had arrived early on purpose to be there before family and friends arrived. He wanted to spend a few last moments alone with his friend. The smell of all the flowers brought back so many memories that it made tears come to his eyes. Most of his family and best friends had been here before they were sent to their graves.

As the old man drew near his friend, he reached out and patted his hand and said in a soft whisper, "You fought long and hard for that last breath, but it was time to give it back, and you won't be in pain anymore."

He then went around to all the flowers, looking for the card that had his name on it. He finally found the flower arrangement and was satisfied with it. As he moved to the back of the room, the old boards creaked beneath his feet. He wearily took a seat over in the dark corner.

Soon, family and friends of the deceased began to filter in to pay their last respects. The old man then saw two of his grandsons come into the room. As soon as the boys saw him, they both made a beeline to his side. He cautioned them to take a seat and to show respect to his old friend.

He had affectionately nicknamed the boys after childhood friends. Stuart, whose nickname was "Snort," was eight years old and Davis, then six years old, was called "Wheezy." The old fellow watched as both little boys were taking in the event as much as they could.

Soon, the circuit was broken, and their questions began to pour out in waves, faster than the old man could answer. "Wait a minute, boys," he said. "Let's do this one at a time."

Wheezy asked first. "How come 'at woman is crying?"

"Well," said the old man slowly, "that was her daddy and she is very sad to lose him."

"What do you mean *lose him*?" asked the young boy.

The old man replied, "Well, let's see . . . look at it this way: Her daddy has finished his long journey."

"What's that mean?" asked Wheezy.

"Wait a minute," Snort declared, "why can't *I* ask a question?"

"Okay, Snort, it's your turn," responded the old man.

"How come them two men are laughing?" questioned Snort.

The old man answered, "The fella' in the brown suit was the man's son. The other fella' was an old friend. I expect they both are remembering something funny that had happened in the past."

The old man, who the boys call Poppy, was beginning to feel like he was on sinking sand. He couldn't keep up.

By this time, Wheezy was getting ready to fire another question, and he had not finished answering his last question. Before Wheezy could get his question out, Snort wanted to know who was the other man talking to the lady. Poppy explained to him that he was the preacher. The preacher, who had a boom-boom voice, was telling the daughter, "I know your father is in heaven, looking down and laughing at this whole affair. He's up there enjoying himself, fishing and catching bass on every cast."

Poppy was amused at the conversation, because just last month, at another funeral, that same preacher had used the same story about a woman singing in "God's choir." But he knew that the preacher was just trying to use words to comfort the man's daughter.

Wheezy was ready for his next question. "Tell me what happened to the man in the big box," he said.

Now Poppy had attended, it seemed, about 500 funerals and had heard about 1,000 sermons preached about this very subject, so he felt he was qualified to answer this question. The old man drew a deep breath and thought to himself, *Now . . . let's see where to start. Well, I have to leave out about what took his life; I don't want to scare them. They won't really understand salvation, and let's see, I can't tell them about his life 'cause they didn't know him.* All of a sudden, he realized *this long journey has a language all its own . . .but* that didn't help him now.

Wheezy was on the edge of his seat, with Snort looking off in the direction of his mom and dad.

"Well, it's sort of like this," Poppy started, as he drew a long breath. "Long ago, Joe was given his first breath when he was born. "

"What does that mean?" asked Wheezy.

"You know what the wind is, don't you?"

"Yes, sir," the lad said.

Poppy continued, "Well, you can't see the wind, but you can see what it does, like the waves on water and blowing leaves, you know."

"Yes, sir," the boy nodded.

"Well, Joe started on his long journey of life—like a trip—and he lived 67 years, until his wind was calmed and he gave the breath back. Now he's lying there up front."

"Uh, huh, is that all?" asked the little boy.

"No, it's not," continued Poppy. "His spirit went to heaven."

"What's spirit?"

"Let's see," said Poppy, "it's that part of him that goes from *here* to *there*. You know what the words here and there mean, don't you?"

"Where's there?" the boy asked.

Poppy replied, "*There* is heaven."

"What's heaven?" was the next question.

"Heaven is a good place that someone paid for a long time ago. It's like someone bought you a ticket to go on a long vacation to a special place. To get to this place, you have to have faith."

The old man had not even gotten that answer out when the next question was fired. "What's faith?"

"Faith is like you know and believe that I'm going to be there and pick you up after school."

The little boy said, "Oh, I see."

Poppy knew he was struggling, trying to get his message across to the boys, when he spied the boys' mother—his daughter-in-law—at the front of the room, watching them. All this deep conversation had not gone unnoticed by the boys' mother, and she began to stroll over to ask Poppy what he was telling them.

"What's going on here?" the boys' mother asked.

With that question, Snort spilled the beans and said, "That man up yonder, in that big box, got his wind knocked out of him and he's gone to heaven on vacation. We'll pick him up after school . . . or something like that."

"Thanks a lot, Snort," the old fellow said.

In an annoyed tone, the boys' mom said, "Hey, we're trying to tell them in a correct way about all this, and all you're going to do is confuse them—like you already have."

"That ain't what Poppy said, Snort," replied Wheezy.

"And another thing," she said, "when they are around you, they talk like they are from another time and place."

"Wait a minute," Poppy said. "Just 'cause I don't sound like I'm a suburbanite from California doesn't mean I didn't try to explain about this thing."

With that, she grabbed the boys by their arms and turned to leave. Wheezy broke free and ran back to the old man. Poppy told the boys that he would do a better job of explaining next time. Wheezy then hugged him good-bye.

Old Poppy had lots of time on his hands now and vowed to figure this whole thing out—not only for the little boys but for himself, as well. His first question was: What's this long journey all about? The longer he thought, the more his question list grew. He wondered why some people accept the end so gracefully and some fight for their wind not to stop. "Wind," he thought out loud. "Now I sound like I'm talking to the boys again." Suddenly, he thought about all the people he had known whose journeys had affected him and others. He couldn't explain any of this. He was dumbfounded that he had been reduced to the mind of a six-year-old child. When you take away all the big words that seemed so shallow to him now, there wasn't much left.

Being very careful to use only the few basic words they had talked about at the funeral home, he began to complete a few lines. As he reviewed what he had written, he thought to himself, *That's plum pitiful, but it's the best I can do.*

It wasn't long before Wheezy came by and Poppy sat him down and pulled out the piece of paper and told him to listen to the answers that he promised him a while back. Poppy asked, "Do you remember?"

"Yes, sir," said the little boy as Poppy began to read.

"When my wind has been calmed and I leave *here* to go *there*, I'll wait for you *there*. And when your wind has been calmed and you leave *here* to go *there*, we'll sit and talk about old times we had together when we were both *here*. But it won't be heaven for me until you're *there*."

The old man knew he would not get much of a response from the boy but hoped that he would understand in 60 years or so. Much to his surprise, the boy looked deep into the old man's eyes and said, "Can I ask a question"?

Oh, no, the old man thought. *Here we go again.* "Okay, ask away."

"Do you promise to wait for me there?"

Startled, Poppy drew the little fellow to him and hugged him tight. "You've got my word, Wheezy," Poppy replied.

The <u>Long Journey</u> really is quite a mystery from the first breath to the last. But I always enjoy a good mystery, don't you?

Poppy

✻ ✻ ✻ ✻ ✻

Children are that part of you that is alive. You watch them grow, laugh and cry—they are why you're here. They grow up and you grow old. After they leave home, they bring joy and pain back into your life when they visit. But upon close examination, they discover there is a parent that died after they first left home.

Poppy '06

The Big Operation

Daddy Bob had promised me that he and I would spend the weekend together. He said we would do a lot of different things. My mother had gone to Ballard County to visit her family, so I got to be with him all weekend. He was through with his obligations as a sailor in World War II and would begin college that fall.

As we were eating breakfast, he was stirring his coffee. He laid the spoon on my hand and said, "Hey, is that too hot to drink?"

Now, Mama Mills always had scalding coffee, so yes, it was hot! I jumped a foot and he laughed so hard he cried. He asked me if I thought it was funny to jump like that. I said, "I guess so," not really believing it.

Daddy Bob then said, "I thought I saw a "gallopin' rod" loose on Old Betsy, the family car." She was really old! A 1938 Chevy and pretty beat up by now. He raised the hood and took a spark plug wire loose and told me to hold it. He needed to see where the gallopin' rod needed to go. He disappeared a minute and fire Old Betsy up. That was the last I remember until I was picking myself up off the ground. My dad was standing over me laughing as hard as he could. "Did you see the gallopin' rod?"

"No, all I saw was a big blue spark."

"Well, now you know where it is, don't you?"

"I sure do," I said with a halfhearted grin.

As we were driving down the road, Daddy Bob said, "Well, I heard Jerry Berry has a couple of monkeys. Would you like to stop and see them?"

"Sure," I said, as we pulled up at the old stockyard in Clinton.

Jerry came out of the office building. It was really an old railroad car that had been turned into an office. It sat next to the stockyard. He had two monkeys with him. One was red, and the other one was black. The red monkey immediately jumped into the back of our old car. When Jerry tried to get the monkey out, she got mad. She then proceeded to take a good healthy crap in the seat. He began to scold her and grabbed at her, but she reached down and got a big handful of crap and threw it at Jerry. Her aim was off, and it hit me right up side the head. A warm green goo slid down the side of my face and onto my tee-shirt. Jimmy Berry, Jerry's younger brother, took me to a hydrant, where the hogs drank, and started cleaning me up.

"Man, that monkey crap really stinks!"

"Yeah, I know," I said, as he took me back to the car.

By now, Jerry had the monkey out of the car. He and my dad were on the ground laughing. Even Jimmy was fighting to keep back a smile.

"Well, we've got to go see Uncle Vester," Daddy Bob announced. Uncle Vester was an old M.D. from World War I days. Long on surgical techniques but short on pain control. While they were chatting, Uncle Vester asked Daddy Bob if he had ever gotten his circumcision operation done.

"Daddy Bob answered, "No."

Uncle Vester said, "You need to be here in the morning (which was Saturday) at 8:00 a.m."

There wasn't any way out, so he agreed to be there.

On the way home, Dad tried to convince me that a circumcision was like having your hair cut or your fingernails clipped. I really think he was trying to convince himself that everything would be alright.

We showed up the next day at 8:00 a.m. Uncle Vester began giving Daddy Bob shots all around his private area. Now, a big old needle stuck there was bound to hurt. But Daddy Bob stood stoic, until a little bead of sweat began to appear on his face. Barely laying the syringe down, the old doc began carving on Daddy Bob. Uncle Vester looked up at me and said he was going to have a frilly dilly, whatever that meant.

A pretty big piece of bloody hide lay on the stainless steel tray. I wasn't very old or experienced at the time, but I knew this was not like any hair cut I had ever seen.

After a whole bunch of stitches were placed, Uncle Vester begin to wrap layer after layer of gauze. It reminded me of a turban that I had seen on a man in a picture show. Finally, Daddy Bob got his new frilly dilly and all the gauze tucked back in his drawers. Uncle Vester had given him six Demerol pills for the pain. "Better take one of these as soon as you can, Robert. This may hurt a little bit." He then looked at me and winked.

We walked by the pool hall. Uncle Lenny, Uncle Clarence and Ralph Bugg told Daddy Bob about a hot pool game that was on for the night. They made him promise to be there at 7:00 p.m. sharp.

"OK, OK, I'll be here," Daddy Bob said with a grin.

Now, the local anesthetics they had back then did not last as long as they do now. So, as we rounded the corner at Brummal's Grocery Store, I noticed Daddy Bob sort of quiver a little. He looked straight ahead and said with a great deal of urgency in his voice, "We've got to get home!"

Daddy Mills rarely drove Old Betsy over 25 miles an hour. But, by the time we reached Harper Hill, she was doing all she could do. Black smoke poured out the back. I remember asking about the galloping rods. "Tain't funny," Daddy Bob said.

When we hit the driveway, there was a big mound of gravel. That's where we lost the muffler. The bumper just caught the corner of the mailbox. It ripped it out of the old milk can, dragging it halfway across the yard. We came to rest just a wee bit short of the front porch, the bumper hanging from just one side now. Steam and smoke came from somewhere under the hood. Daddy Bob was nowhere in sight. As I got out and ran inside, I saw Daddy Bob at the cistern, drawing water.

Daddy Bob was the type that thought if one pill was good, two would be better, but three would fill the bill. Three Demerols will do quite a number on even a grown man. In 30 minutes, he quit moaning and holding himself and was fast asleep.

At five that afternoon, Daddy Bob woke up and was getting ready for the big pool game. He began unwrapping all the gauze covering the wound. The bulge in his pants was a distraction to him, he said.

As we were driving back to town, he told me a funny story. It had happened a week earlier. The story goes: Uncle Lenny was probably the worst pool shot in all the county. But he loved to play. (If there was really such a thing as a leprechaun, it would be a picture of Uncle Lenny.) It seems that Daddy Bob and Uncle Lenny were playing pool. Daddy Bob was going to break the balls. Uncle Lenny got down low at the opposite end and said, "You can't break worth a shit, Robbie."

Well, with that, Daddy Bob drew back and hit the Q ball as hard as he could. It immediately skipped over the rack of balls and hit Uncle Lenny square between the eyes, knocking him down and out. By the time Daddy Bob got to Uncle Lenny's stretched out body, a knot as big as a hen egg jumped up between his eyes. As soon as Uncle Lenny came to, he began to rub his new-found knot. When Daddy Bob could see that he was going to be alright, he asked Uncle Lenny, "How's your little knot?"

Now, I believed all the story but knew Daddy Bob was probably laughing his head off. I admit it probably was really very funny. But, as the old story goes, the sun shines on every old dog's ass sometimes. Uncle Lenny would get his turn on down the road.

It had rained that Saturday afternoon, and it was so hot and steamy you could hardly breathe. We crossed in front of Brummel's Grocery on our way over to the pool hall. I can still remember the smell of Pop Johnson's hamburgers cooking. There the pool tables were, all in a row, all the way to the rear of the old shotgun building. Daddy Bob said to Pop, "Get the boy a hamburger?"

"What does he want on it?"

"Just run it through the garden," Daddy Bob said smiling, as he picked up a cue stick from the rack.

Mr. Johnson asked, "What to drink, boy?"

"Well, how 'bout one of those big ol' orange drinks," I said.

"Coming right up," was his answer.

Uncle Clarence and Tight-Eye Bugg were already partners. This left Daddy Bob with poor old Uncle Lenny. Now, even though they were partners, Uncle Lenny got down in his stance and said, "You still can't shoot for shit, Robbie."

With that, Daddy Bob waved his stick in the air and said, "Get out of the way, Lenny! I would hate to make that knot pop back up again. By the way, how's your little knot?"

As he waved the cue in the air, it accidentally hit the corner of the table. It sailed high in the air. When it came down, the big thick end fell . . . you guessed it . . .right on the business end of his new frilly dilly—you know, the part where he had removed the gauze, so it wouldn't bulge.

I had always been told the Mills clan had come from Ireland and Scotland. I guess it was so 'cause Daddy Bob started out, as he circled the pool table, with an old Irish Jig. He reached the other side and did a Scottish Fling. When he finally got to the end of the table, he finished with his own rendition of the famous River Dance. Clutching up his whole frilly dilly with both hands, the blood began to pour. He slouched in a row of seats at the end of the table. Slowly, Uncle Lenny strolled over and got down real close and said to Daddy Bob, "How's that little knot of yours now, Robbie?"

Well, the whole place exploded with laughter. After a few minutes, Daddy Bob grabbed my hand and said, "We've got to get home!"

Grabbing my burger and big orange, we were soon at the front door. Mr. Johnson called out, "Enos Slaughter is up to bat with the bases loaded. Ain't you gonna hear how the game turns out?"

I've seen some pretty bad stares in my time, but I swear my daddy's eyes were shooting fire. He fired Old Betsy up. This time, she was going full out at the north end of town. Somewhere around Luther Lampkin's place, the needle on the speedometer just fell off the dial. We hit what was left of the small pile of gravel at the turn. We lost the muffler again. My granddaddy had wired it back on from the first time. The mailbox can had been put back. The bumper hooked it again and drug the mailbox and the milk can right up to the front door.

Somehow I knew where to find Daddy Bob after the smoke had cleared. He was at the cistern gulping down those last three pills. Next morning, Daddy Mills wired on what was left of the bumper. He just gave up on the muffler. Old Betsy never really recovered from the pool game. For nearly two months, 'til the new muffler came in from Montgomery Ward, people could hear us crank Old Betsy up all the way to Shiloh.

Before Daddy Bob went to sleep that night, he sat on the side of the bed. He placed all the gauze back on his new frilly dilly.

My dad always tried to tell me that there is something funny in just about everything. I guess that's true 'cause I've been a great source of entertainment for myself—just by laughing at all the boo-boos I've pulled.

As my long journey comes to an end, what I would give to hear him say, "Hey, Jerry boy, is that too hot to drink?" Not the galloping rod deal—that just hurt too much.

Thanks for all the laughs, Daddy Bob!
Poppy

"We'll Leave The Light On For You"

Richard pulled out on the highway early one morning, going to work. As he eased down the road, he fiddled with the radio dial, and the familiar words of Tom Bodett came over the speaker, "This is Tom Bodett speaking for Motel 6. We'll leave the light on for you."

Richard always liked to hear those words; it reminded him of home when he was a teenager. As he thought about home, he began to remember his mom and dad and how they had raised him to be a man. Church was always first, family and friends second, do your best, and all the rest will take care of itself. He remembered the tough times when he was very young, but God had always pulled them through. Richard felt very lucky to have been blessed to have parents like his.

Richard and his wife Sandy had a son Clifton who meant the world to the couple. Both Richard and his wife made a vow to try and be good parents and to follow the road map his mom and dad had made for him. That very day, as Richard came home from work, he drove by Mayberry's Antique Store. He stopped in to browse around and shoot the breeze with the owner who told him to just look around 'til he finished doing a little business with a customer.

As Richard strolled up one musty-smelling aisle and down the other, he spied a couple of old "coal oil" lamps way back in a dusty corner.

"Hey, do those old lamps work?" Richard asked.

"Yeah," a reply echoed back. "But there's a story about those old lamps," the owner said as he came up behind Richard.

"What's the story?" asked Richard.

"Well, it seems an old woman during the Civil War lit those lamps every night for her son until he came safely home. After the war was over, the young man told his mother that he could close his eyes and envision her lighting those lamps so he could find his way home. . . You know how old people can tell stories and make them sound true or make you think they are true."

Both Richard and the owner laughed. Just as Richard turned to leave, he asked, "Hey, how much do you want for those old lamps?"

"Well," the owner stated, "they have been here as long as I've owned the store, so it's not like they are a hot item. I'll tell you what I'll do. I'll sell them both for . . .say . . .$10."

"Hmm," Richard muttered to himself.

With that, the owner said he would throw in the box of wicks. "That's enough there to last at least 500 years."

"Yeah, I bet," replied Richard. "Let me look." Sure enough, the box was full. "Well, I think I'll take them," Richard said with a sigh.

As he loaded the lamps and the big box of wicks into the back of his pickup truck, he mumbled to himself, "Now what am I going to do with these two old lamps? My wife will wring my neck for bringing this junk home."

Then he had an idea. *If I were to place them in the windows on either side of the front door and light them each night, it would be like that ad on the radio I like so well. But,* he thought, *it's got to mean more than that. Maybe lighting the lamps would honor my parents for having a light on for me when I was a young boy. Also, as I light the lamps, it would be symbolic that I was trying to live correctly in my faith and daily living, by letting my light shine. Maybe, in some way, it would be symbolic in guiding my son home.*

Richard sat down that very night and explained his feelings about lighting the lamps every night to his wife. This would be something they would do with each other along with their boy. He also explained that some day one of the lamps would be passed on to the boy.

From that day on, the lamps were lit every night. Even though the light from the small lamps was very dim, the ritual burned deep into the little boy's heart.

Eighteen years later, a war is going on and Clifton is far away in that war. At home, as night begins to fall, Richard and his wife light the first lamp. For some unknown reason, Richard takes the second lamp down from the window sill.

"What are you doing?" asked his wife.

"It's time to give one away," he replied.

It's Christmas, and even though they know Clifton can't come home, they place the lamp under the Christmas tree.

"We promised each other that someday when Clifton grew up to be a man, we would give him one of the lamps. I think that day has arrived," Richard said. "He's not due to come home for Christmas, but I think we need to put something under the tree for him."

So they wrapped the lamp and placed it under the tree.

Later that very night, a car came around the corner. It was their boy, who, at the last minute, had gotten a furlough. As a surprise, he had not called to tell them he was coming home for Christmas. Fully expecting to see the two small lights in the window, as he had seen all his life, there was only one. Many thoughts raced through his mind . . .*Was one broken? . . .Was it out of oil? . . . Or maybe Dad or Mom were sick or even worse.*

As he raced to the door, they saw him coming! Oh! What a happy reunion. The first words he said after he caught his breath were, "Where's the other lamp?"

Richard nodded toward the package under the tree and said, "It's your turn now. Remember, Mom and I said when you were older one of the lamps would be yours."

The boy took the lamp and placed it back in the window and lit the wick. "When I get my house, I'll put it in the front window, just like home," he said with a smile.

Richard asked, "Son, when you light your lamp every night, what do you think that represents?"

The boy thought for a minute and said, "When all those shells were exploding around me and friends were dying, I would close my eyes and think about home. I couldn't recognize your faces and everything seemed blurry, but I could see those two small lit lamps as clear as if I was standing in our front yard. You asked what they represent—they represent my past, the present and the future. When I light my lamp in my house, it will be for the next generation to find their way home."

"That's good enough, son," Richard replied.

I bid you farewell,

Poppy

Going Home Is A Little Dusty Now

I would like to let you in on a little secret of mine. Well, really it's a small theory I have. Some time ago, I started searching for a way back home. I found that all routes seem to start with the same history, and I began to write down secrets that I harbored from when I was a kid.

My story begins when my parents left me, during my formative years, with my grandparents. They lived on a small farm in far western Kentucky, so when I refer to home, that's the place I mean.

I have been around several orphans in my life, and even though I'm not one, I have felt, in some small way, the feelings of being left and holding onto the surrogate folks left in charge but still longing for that missing link that suddenly left my life, only to reappear ever' so often. This little play went on for several years, until one day, they came for me and I had to leave home.

Now, many years have passed, and as I stand before row after row of granite stones with deep cuts in them, telling their names and dates, I walk away with a feeling of being lost. How could I ever go home without them?

I find myself standing in the middle of the Home Place . . .you know, where my old home once stood. It is gone now, never to come back. How can I go home? Suddenly, I feel a cold shiver go down my bones—they're all gone. Even my house is gone. How can I go home?

Home is now a memory, stuck on some lonely, dusty shelf in the museum of my mind. I realize I can never really go home again. Sometimes, though, I can shake the dust from these old memories, and for a short time, I fool myself and go back there. Someday, when you reach my age, you may also rediscover your dusty home.

I miss them more every day—those folks from my past and that old farmhouse. To me that will always be Home, but then I can never really go home, can I?

Poppy

* * * * *

This story is a simple one about my childhood days and home. When we lose our innocence, loved ones and the house we lived in, things suddenly become complicated. If you inject your past as a reader into the framework of the story, it too will become convoluted and twisted. Sometimes, simplicity can become very complicated, don't you think?

Understanding Special Pain

I know this won't be a popular story. It isn't funny in any way. However, I did feel compelled to write it anyway. Hopefully, it will mean something to some or just a few. Maybe it will mean something to only one, and that one is who this story is for.

We all have pain throughout our lives; that's what makes it so special when we're not in pain. Sore throats, earaches, headaches and, heaven forbid, a toothache are bad, but as bad as they hurt, they are usually temporary. I'm not writing about those kinds of pain; I'm writing about pains that I think are special . . . pain like someone screaming about the pain in their mind and then ends their life, leaving us a good measure of pain and questions about ourselves. One question we ask ourselves: "Why didn't I see this coming?" That special pain is of guilt.

Maybe the pain concerns the loss of a child in pain. That goes with you to the grave. This is like the pictures I get each month from St. Jude's Childrens Hospital showing innocent children sick and dying from a disease I can do nothing about. A very special pain, don't you think?

Maybe seeing two old people, who have worked hard all their lives, sitting around a table wondering what foods to give up so they can pay for their prescription drugs. They are too proud to ask for help.

I was once on staff at a rest home and saw a family bringing their dad in. They said their good-byes and told him that they would come and visit. The family sold his farm, his house, and divided the spoils.

Each day the old man would get dressed and tell the housekeeper his family was coming to see him that day, but at sundown he would always say, "They'll be here tomorrow." They never came. This went on for two years.

On his final day, the old man got dressed and told the housekeeper, like always, that his family was coming to visit him that day. He waited until sunset. No one came. The housekeeper turned the old man's linens down and fluffed his pillows. She told him that maybe they would come tomorrow.

"No," he spoke softly, "this was the last day."

She left to get her supper, but when she returned, the old man was gone. A very special pain to bear, don't you think—to die alone?

Picture a son, holding his mother close, for the last time. She is dying of terminal cancer. All his tears are gone. All the words, he thinks, have been said. But as he stands there, words come from deep inside of him. He turns to her and says, "I'm so sorry for your pain." Then there was a loss for words again—just a blank spot. A small smile came across her face, and he finished saying, "I will love you forever."

I know about that pain all too well. I was that son. After all these years, I have thought and studied about that blank. As I wrote these words, it was like a blinding light that suddenly struck me between the eyes. Her smile meant, "I understand." I had finally filled in the blank.

Like I said at the beginning, these words may not mean much to many, but I think they might mean something to one special person. I may not ever get to meet you, but if I could, I would softly whisper these words in your ear, "I'm so sorry for your pain. I understand and I will love you forever."

I bid you farewell,
Poppy

Spit In the Devil's Eye

I take my breaks in the morning by walking to the grave of an old friend, Dr. Steele Robbins. I make this pilgrimage each day that I'm at the office, weather permitting.

Dr. Robbins practiced medicine in the building next to mine, and I had known him for nearly 50 years now. He would take his break and visit me as I would do the same. We became close friends.

As I look down at the bronze plaque that marks his grave, it doesn't tell anything about the man I knew as my friend. I remember the things the preacher said about him, as I helped carry him to his final resting place that day. All the people's assessments and thoughts about my old friend puzzled me because they didn't include any of my experiences with him at all.

Steele was a brilliant surgeon and a great internist. To me he was the sharpest tack in the box. He also excelled as a great shot and knowledgeable fisherman. We had both been biology and chemistry majors in college, so we looked at the world maybe from a little different slant than most. We often talked about wolves, coyotes, buzzards and opossum. We simply referred to them as morticians of nature and, in some degree, had a lot of respect for these critters.

One time, as I had just gotten back from a caribou hunting trip along the Arctic, he came into the back door of my office, announcing his presence the same way he had done 1,000 times before: "Hey, you old shit, where are you?" I soon told him about my trip and what I saw concerning wolves.

I had taken a nice bull caribou late one afternoon and had field dressed it before heading back to camp. I had noticed a lone wolf atop a distant rise but thought nothing of it.

The next day, the Indian who was running the boat said he wanted to show me something. As we walked to where the caribou carcass was, there was literally nothing left. Where did it go? "Wolves," he said with a smile. "Clean" was all he said.

Steele seemed to like the story and soon left.

A few weeks went by and I got a phone call from Steele for me to come by his home for a visit. It was late when I went by to see him. There was only a single light on in his den. We talked for a while and then he tossed a pathology report in my direction. I soon read about his cancer—the type, grade and where it had spread. I started to say something when he placed his finger to his mouth for me to be quiet. He looked over his right shoulder and spoke in the direction of the darkest part of the room.

"Now, be quiet boys, it won't be much longer . . . but I've got a surprise for you . . . all the best pieces have been eaten."

It took me by surprise, and I laughed out loud. I could almost make out a pack of wolves waiting back in the dark. He had really fooled me.

Then he said to me in a very serious tone, "Never miss an opportunity to spit in the devil's eye."

I guess if I could add something to that plaque that marks Steele's grave for all the people who knew him, it would be that he was one of a kind.

I think back on all the house calls I went on with Steele, knowing there would probably be no pay. He would simply say I have to go and I understand. He was one of a kind right to the very end.

So, if you see me trudging toward the graveyard, you'll know I'm taking a break to go and visit my old friend. Some days, as the wind murmurs through the magnolia tree that stands guard over his grave, I swear sometimes the wind sounds like Steele's voice as it says, "Is that you, you old shit?"

Jerry Mills, DMD

The Ritual

My wife and I were driving to Nicky's Bar-B-Q Restaurant, a few miles north of Clinton, Kentucky, a few weeks ago to pick up six fresh hams. As we went through Fulgham, I asked her if she had ever heard the story that Harrison Keillor told on his radio show Prairie Home Companion about "hog-killin'. She said she had not heard about it. So I told her the story as best I remember.

After thanking Nicky for getting the hams, he said in a slow drawl, "You know, Doc, you could have gotten some already cured back toward town, with half the bother."

"Yeah, I know, " I said, smiling, "but it wouldn't be the same."

Turning toward the homeplace, my thoughts turned back to a simpler and more comfortable time in my life.

I was about five years old when I witnessed the whole process that occurred every November when cold weather stayed for a while. The process started a few days before the *Ritual* was in full bloom, getting the scalding trough clean and firewood placed under the trough. Then the trough was filled with water, all in preparation for the big event.

Everyone arrived about 7:00 a.m.—Uncle Clyde and his wife; Cousin Luther along with his wife and two daughters; Uncle Ben and his tribe; and of course, Mama and Daddy Mills. Most of the clan had two hogs per family.

Uncle Clyde was the best shot of the bunch, so he was selected to do the killin'. Seems that Daddy Mills had tried his hand one time and missed the right spot, hitting the hog in the snout. Uncle Clyde had to finish the job. That day would be Daddy Mills' last chance because, with a smile, everyone would say, "Don't let Albert shoot my hog!" That would be the only time that day I would hear or see any smiling or laughter. The whole process would turn very somber.

This was a very serious occasion. Thinking back, it had to be serious because outside of chickens, a few squirrels and ducks that Uncle Clyde dropped off, pork was the only other meat anyone had.

I would stick my fingers in my ears and look away as each hog was shot and placed in the boiling water. The hogs were then strung up high in the air, held by a singletree, a harness on a wagon and a rope tied to a nearby tree. After a prescribed time, the hog was shaved of its hair and cut up into different pieces. Some of the pieces were taken to the kitchen where the women of each family processed it into sausage, ribs and scraps. The scraps made souse meat—farm folks' lunch meat. The guts were made into chittlins.

Cracklins were made outside by the men folks. Bacon slabs, hams and shoulders were left to cool before placing in salt boxes to cure. Each family seemed to differ on the length of time the meat was to stay in the salt, but all seemed happy with their results.

Daddy Mills would rub all the joints and knuckles of the meat with salt to make sure the meat would cure properly. Then he would lift me over into the salt box, and I would place new meat salt over the hams, shoulders and bacon slabs. At a later time, we would smoke the meat.

It has been 65 years ago now, and my immediate family place our hams and bacon in our salt box to get ready to smoke the meat with hickory chips some (secret) days later—just like in my childhood. I know that I have fulfilled my part of our family's *Ritual*.

Every late fall, when the air is crisp and I hear the sound of geese on their fall migration, I think of those days long ago when our neighbors, friends and family were so dependent on each other. Those days are long gone. However, I still have the warm memories of my kids, grandkids and my wife spending many hours together curing and smoking our hams and bacon.

Now I guess Wal-Mart can't sell memories, can they?

Poppy

* * * * *

As I sat listening to Garrison Keillor's radio show, while watching the glowing coals in my fireplace, I find myself eagerly awaiting the news from Lake Wobegon. Some of the news is about current events and about things that most folks can relate to. But ever' so often, he reflects on things of his past, things of his childhood. So many of these stories are very parallel with my childhood.

Even though Mr. Keillor is a famous and complicated man, I somehow think in my mind that he longs for a simpler time in his life. When he finishes his news from Lake Wobegon, it reminds me of a time when family, friends and neighbors were so much more than they seem today.

As Mr. Keillor ends his story, he always says, "That's the news from lake Wobegon where all the children are above average, all the women are strong (most women from Minnesota are big and strong and not very pretty), and all the men are good-looking." I always laugh and think about Springhill, Kentucky, where all the children are above average, the women are good-looking and the men are strong.

I'm sure most readers like to slip off in their minds—somewhere it's quiet, warm and cozy, a place where they are happy with others and themselves. We all have our special *Rituals*, don't you think?

Poppy

Richard's Vacation

I never tire of old stories about sons and their daddies. Some sons have a bond with their daddy that's so strong the mere mention of his name or a thought from the past brings a tear to their eyes or a break in their voice or both. I have a friend who told me a story about such a bond. The story goes something like this . . .

On a small farm in the hills of Arkansas, a long time ago, a son and his daddy would come onto their farm each day and walk and talk about the events of the day. On one particular walk, as they neared the top of a hill, the daddy stopped and placed his hand on his son's shoulder and said, "You know, we're mighty lucky."

"How's that, Daddy?" the boy asked.

"Well, son, we get to come here to walk and talk. Why, it's like having a little vacation every day."

The son turned to his dad and said, "Why, you're right, Daddy, you're right."

I've heard that story on several occasions and it never varies, but I think my friend forgot to tell me the final chapter of the story. It might go something like this . . .

After they are reunited someday, they will stroll again on that same old farm, but this time, as they reach the top of the hill, the son will stop and place his hand on his daddy's shoulder and say these words, "You know, Daddy, we're really lucky."

His daddy asks, "How's that, son?"

The son answers, "We get to come here to walk and talk and have a little vacation every day, but the best part is this vacation will <u>never</u> end!"

The daddy replies, "You're right, son, you're right."

And they stroll over the hill, talking about the events of the day.

In the past, I have lost family members and friends that I was always too embarrassed to tell them how much I cared for them. I have promised myself I would not let that happen again, so my humble chapter to your <u>great</u> story is my way of saying, "I love and appreciate you."

Your friend,
Jerry

Memories of the Ol' Poppy Pitch

At the Triple A, for 13-year-old boys' baseball World Series in Kansas City, Missouri, Brad Trease leaned over to me and said that I needed to write a story about the Poppy Pitch and our team the Outlaws. I laughed and said it would surely be a short story, and we both laughed about that.

As I looked at the empty mound, I thought the story might go something like this . . .

As the old man stared at the pitcher's mound, he thought back to when he was about 10 years old and was pitching off a mound like that. He remembered his fast ball, a two seamer that wasn't all that fast. But he had a pitch he had dreamed up that worked pretty well.

Sixty years later, he had taught that same pitch to his grandson Stewart. The old man had watched Stewart win many games using that same pitch. He also remembered teaching the pitch to a young boy named Payton whose baseball coach had given up on his pitching. Now, Payton was pitching in a World Series game, and the old coach was nowhere to be found.

The old fellow watched the coaches preparing for the upcoming game to start. He laughed to himself about how Coach Tim was always out of the dugout wandering through the crowd and Coach Brad was always sucking up to the umpires. He watched Coach Steve looking for the line-up, while Coach P was cracking off a toot to loosen up the kids.

Tammy, our scorekeeper, was busy looking for the 12th line on the line-up sheet when Mrs. English nudged the old man on the shoulder and issued an order for him to go and give the boys a pep talk. She said that they wouldn't listen to her. She told him that the boys would listen to him.

After making his way to the dugout, he told them the same things he had always said but with a little more urgency in his voice this time. But he did grab Payton's arm as he left to pitch. "Make that Ole Poppy Pitch hop for me, Payton."

"I'll do my best," Payton said with a smiling face, and hop it did!

As Coach Tim called the last pitch, he leaned over in the direction of the old man and softly said, "This pitch is for you, Poppy."

"You're out!" cried the umpire, as the ball crossed the plate.

"Well, it would have meant a little more if Payton had not thrown 25 Poppy Pitches in a row," said the old man.

It was one of the few times that he had seen Coach Tim laugh that long and hard.

The last game came up and our star pitcher Seth had pitched his last inning. He strolled up to where the old man was seated and said, grinning, "Did you see the look on that kid's face when that Poppy Pitch froze him?"

"Yeah, that was great," the old man said, remembering back 60 years ago when he had seen that same look on opposing batters' faces.

Well, we lost the game and the old man shuffled back to the car to leave when that scrawny, snot-nosed kid that still dwelt somewhere deep inside him turned and looked back at the empty ballpark. He uttered these words to himself, "We may not have won the World Series, but we sure scared the shit out of ya'!" He then reached into his pocket and turned an old baseball and said to himself, "Maybe we can find a new wrinkle or twist to that Ol' Poppy Pitch. After all, we've got several months before the Outlaws ride again."

Poppy

The Cleansing

It was a time of great strife in our country. It was the time of the great depression, when the pay was 50 cents for a hard day's work, if you could even find a job.

My Uncle Lenny ran a county road crew for Hickman County, KY. The crew fixed bridges on county roads. My daddy was one of the crew members, along with Arley, a black man named Vince, and finally a big ol' fat, lazy man who went by the name of Clabber Head.

The story unfolds as the old work truck pulled up in front of Clabber's house. Well, it really wasn't a truck but was a make-shift, homemade version of a truck. It consisted of an A-model Ford with a wooden bed bolted on the back. It had a wooden cab, of sorts, over the driver. Now Clabber Head's house had never seen a fresh coat of paint in over 20 years. There was just a little trace of white paint left here and there that had not peeled off.

Underneath the house was open so you could see through. There were a good many chickens that lived under there. Also, there were several goats resting on the front porch. There was an old maple tree in the front yard with five or six half-naked kids swinging on an old hemp rope hanging from a limb. There was an assortment of all kinds of dogs lying half asleep in the shade of the old tree.

Right next to the house was a small pond that served a half dozen hogs as a good place to "waller" and cool off from the hot July sun.

Old Clabber Head waddled toward the truck, all 325 pounds. He had alunch pail filled with a dozen cat-head biscuits and a half-gallon tin full of Uncle Ben's sorghum molasses. His dinner was always the same except for what he could scrounge off his fellow workers. He always dressed the same—no shirt, bibbed overalls, and a pair of Brogan shoes with no laces or socks.

As he sat the cheeks of his butt on the back of the truck bed, the old springs creaked. The whole bed of the truck sagged under the weight of old Clabber Head. This particular day, he had a sack filled with half-grown, sore-eyed cats. He planned to dump the cats in the first creek they crossed.

I guess that was quite a sight as the little road crew pulled away on its way to an old fallen-down bridge down the winding, dusty road. When they came to the first creek, a good mile or so down the road, old Clabber Head threw the sack full of the squalling, fighting cats off the side and down into the ditch. No one had noticed except Uncle Lenny.

They got to the bridge that was due to have some new sill put in. Uncle Lenny got everything squared away, then told everyone he had forgotten some tools. He said he would be back in a little while. Soon he was back to where the sack had been thrown out. He quickly gathered it up and placed it by him in the cab of the old truck. When he got near Clabber Head's house, he untied the sack, and all the cats scampered home. He then drove back and deposited the sack, minus the cats, where Clabber had thrown them. He then returned to the crew at the bridge.

This routine continued for six or seven trips that summer until Clabber Head finally gave up trying to get rid of the cats. By that time, Uncle Lenny had convinced Clabber Head that the cats were really super smart. They were able to untie that sack from the inside and to find their way home.

"I just can't 'figger' it out, how they can untie that sack," Clabber would say.

Uncle Lenny would chime in and tell him that he could probably sell those cats for as much as a dollar apiece.

"Think so, Lenny?" Clabber asked.

"Sure. Why don't you put up a sign. I bet there's at least 20 or so people that go by your house every day. Why, I bet they would be gone in no time at all."

Sure enough, the next day, as the crew pulled up to Clab's house, there a sign tacked on the old maple tree. It read: Super Cats for Sale. $1 apiece.

Uncle Lenny told him he bet that two or three of those cats would sell while they were at work that day. "If all those cats have kittens, you'll probably be able to retire by fall," said Uncle Lenny, trying to keep a straight face.

Of course, no one bought any of the cats, but by summer's end, one thing did happen. All the cats had kittens, and now they numbered in the low 90s.

It seems that old Clabber Head had a really bad habit. He would sidle up close to a crew member after he had gulped down his biscuits and sorghum. As the crew member was finishing his dinner, Clabber would roll out a loud, wet toot that would "singe the hair on your nose." Clabber would then ask, "Hey, you want that half of sandwich?"

Half gagging, the fellow would say, "Here, take it. I can't stand the smell anymore."

Uncle Lenny had been watching this happen over the course of the summer. He went to my dad and said, "I've got a plan on how we can stop those toots."

"How's that?" Dad asked.

"Well, if we pool a little money, we'll buy some ExLax." Uncle Lenny then proceeded to tell him the plan.

They saved all week long, got their ducks in a row, and when Monday morning came, the plan went into stage one. Around ten that morning, Uncle Lenny let the crew take a little break. My dad whipped out a big ExLax bar that looked like a Hershey chocolate bar. He began to unwrap the foil off the candy. When Clabber spied my dad going to take a bite, he sidled up close. He let out a big wet one and let out a giggle.

"Whoa!" said my dad. He then started to wrap the foil back over the bar.

"Hey, how about a little of that chocolate?" says old Clabber.

"Here, take it. I think I'm going to be sick," replied my dad.

The plan had worked! Ol' Clab downed that whole bar in a couple of seconds. As he sat with his mouth full of ExLax, Uncle Lenny and Dad had little grins on their faces. Stage two was only a couple of hours away.

Uncle Lenny and Dad had gotten my grandmother to make a chocolate pie the night before. Before the meringue was made, they ground up another bar of ExLax and sprinkled it on top of the chocolate filling. For good measure, they put a few drops of castor oil here and there.

All of this went unnoticed by my near-sighted grandmother, as she then put the meringue over the whole concoction.

It took about one half hour before the big rumble began to start. But when it started, boy did things change for Clabber.

"Hey, Lenny, where's that roll of paper?" Clabber hollered.

"Under the seat," answered Lenny.

"Lenny, whose pie is that on the seat?" inquired Clabber.

"Why, it belongs to Robert. Maybe he'll give you some at dinner."

Clabber never heard a word. He was gone, as the flood gates were just beginning to open. Well, ol' Clab went through that roll of toilet paper in about 15 minutes and was asking Lenny for some more. Lenny told him that was all they had. He would have to use some leaves.

Clab must have wiped on half the leaves in the woods. He declared, "I'm so sore I can't stand to touch my behind."

By this time, he couldn't get his bib overalls down fast enough. It was running down both legs, so he took out his pocket knife and cut the bottom out of his pants. This exposed his big, fat, red, raw butt for all the world to see.

When things began to slow down a bit, it was dinner time. Clabber sidled up next to my dad and asked for a sliver of that chocolate pie. He smelled so bad my dad said, "Here, take it all." With a big smile, Clab began to eat the whole pie. Sure 'nuf, in about 15 minutes, the show started all over again.

Ol' Clab went through pure hell that hot August afternoon. His butt got redder and redder and rawer and rawer. Uncle Lenny announced that they were going to call it quits for the day around three o'clock. Ol' Clab was a little under the weather, he told everyone.

When they got close to Clab's house, Clabber jumped off the back of that old truck and started off for the hog waller hole that was next to his house. He didn't slow down at the gate but proceeded to jump over a split-rail fence. Well, he didn't quite make it over the top rail. He hung his foot, tooted and pooted at the same time.

"Whooee, not a pretty sight," Lenny said with a slight chuckle.

By now, all the men were down on the floor of the truck, howling with laughter. Ol' Clab finally made it to waller hole and jumped in, butt and all.

That was the last day my dad worked for the Hickman County bridge crew. About a week later, Uncle Lenny came by with six cans of sorghum. He told my dad that Clab had sent them to him but warned him not to eat a lot at once. They might give you the runs.

You see, Clabber Head thought the molasses was a little "green." "I'm laying off them for life. My bowels still ain't right," said Clab.

Poppy

Boundary Waters

It was about time for me to go to Canada on our family's annual fishing trip. It would be my 40th trip and my oldest son's 38th trip, while my grandson had tagged along five times. We go to an area that is set aside for campers and canoeists, where there are no boats or motors and where cans, bottles or anything not disposable isn't allowed. It's some 30 miles from the last Indian village. Cell phones don't work there at all. It is a wilderness area that sits, in my opinion, on top the very best smallmouth bass fishing in the world.

I was in a big outdoor store in Paducah, picking up some last-minute tackle when a salesman came up to me and said, "Hey, old timer, need some help? Couldn't help but notice you over in the light tackle section. You looking for something for your grandkids?"

"No," I said, "I just like ultra-light stuff."

The salesman replied, "Come over here and get some man-size stuff . . . something you can cross their eyes with."

I tried to tell him where I was headed, but it never registered with him. He kept referring to how he always fished out of the front of the boat, drinking beer. He continued telling me how he always used heavy bass tackle. I told him, as politely as I could, to just let me kill a little time looking. At that, he started to move on toward the next customer. Looking back over his shoulder, he called to me and said, "I'm looking to go on the Tournament Circuit soon, and that "girly" tackle just won't work for that, old timer."

I was soon forgotten as the salesman approached the next guy and asked, "Hey, buddy, looking for tackle to cross those eyes? Well—" and he didn't get to finish his statement as I walked off but could still hear the conversation.

The customer said he was interested in what I had to say, but the salesman said in a low gruff voice, "That simple old man wants to fish with kids' stuff . . . Say, you know much about tournament fishing?"

"Some," the man stated. "I've been doing it for about three years now. I've kind of lost some of my desire."

"Well," said the salesman, "I run a Ranger boat and a 250 HP engine and I've got three or four years' experience under my belt. I'm going to give it a try . . . big money, you know."

The man left the salesman standing and talking and came up to me and told me his name. He began asking questions about the Boundary Waters in Canada and ultra-light tackle. He told me that he had lost a lot of his desire to fish.

"Well," I said, "I think ultra-light fishing will bring that back."

On my advice, he bought a G-Loomis ultra-light rod and ultra-light spinning reel with 4-lb. test line. He also bought a bunch of small lures that I had suggested. As we left the fishing area, we both overheard the salesman approach a new customer and say, "Hey, you looking for something to cross ol' Billy Bass's eyes? Come here and see what I use . . . Say, did I fail to mention I'm thinking about being a Pro Bass man and going on the Circuit?"

The man and I just looked at each other, smiled and left the store together, chatting about past fishing experiences. Three days later, I was waving good-bye to the Indian who had dropped us off at the bottle portage going into Quetico National Park. It would be the last time I would see or hear anyone else for a week, outside my son and grandson.

The ice had been gone for a couple of weeks, and it had been raining for several weeks straight. The temperature was very cold. It had been in the low 90's when we left home but was a brisk 48 degrees here. As I grabbed one of the seven packs we had brought and started up a steep, rocky, muddy trail, I was suddenly attacked by what seemed like every black fly and mosquito in Canada. Brad, my son, had already left before me, carrying the canoe and paddles, with his son Stuart. Stuart was also packing a huge pack.

The portage was about 80 rods long—not all that far—but after two or three trips over and back, with packs that weigh 65-70 pounds, it can get a little rough. After all the gear was carried over the trail, we were ready for the long paddle to the campsite.

As we pushed off from the bank in the loaded canoe, we were met with a 25 mile-an-hour wind right in our face. The air smelled of pine, and the water was gin clear. After a paddle of 4.5 miles, we finally decided that a sheltered bay on the east side of the lake would be the best spot to set up camp.

After pitching the tent and stowing all our gear, we decided to catch just enough fish to eat during our stay and release everything else. We paddled to where a small stream entered the lake and began catching walleye—2-3 pounds each—as fast as the tiny gigs would reach the bottom. In 45 minutes, we had caught 75 or so fish. I began to fillet about 15 fish. Now, 30 good fillets will go a long way for just three people.

Back at the camp, we grilled a nice steak apiece, which we ate with a baked potato and a spinach salad. We then turned in for the night. Even though it was 10:30 p.m., it was still light outside.

A huge storm hit during the night, and it rained all night and all the next day until just about dark. While it was still light, we eased the canoe through a big headwind for 2-3 miles, where we finally got to Peterson Bay. Now the bay had warmed up to 60 degrees, just right for smallmouth bass to start spawning.

It was a great feeling to hold the canoe for two great fishermen. They fished until dark and released at least 100 bass that put up some of the best aerial displays I could ever remember.

I was completely worn out after eating Walleye fillets and all the trimmings. As I lay in my sleeping bag, listening to the lonesome call of a loon right in front of our camp, and its mate calling back somewhere in the darkness, I couldn't help but think about things at home—another world so different from the world I was in now. Things that were so important a week ago were far away and unimportant here. In a weird way, both worlds were completely apart but also alike—a dog-eat-dog world at home but a survival world here.

As I reflected on the day, I saw a dad who was a masterful fisherman softly teaching all his skills to his son—like I had done for him so long ago. I watched them send their tiny lures toward the haunts of so many smallmouth bass that afternoon. They would skillfully entice a strike and then, on that light angel-hair line, gently bring them to the canoe, only to release them and watch them swim away. There wasn't a cheer or a high five, only a nod in appreciation of a duel between two chess players—a deadly serious game for the fish but only fun for the angler.

I thought of the salesman whose tackle greatly over-matched the fish, with all the odds totally in his favor and with money as the reward. I wondered how he would fare with the big cheeks of his butt hanging over the gunnel of that small canoe and with that big line that the fish could see and not bite his lure . . . how a day without his ration of beer while fishing out of a $50,000 bass boat would be. Not so hot, I thought to myself.

None of these things mattered here—only the simple things. Yes, I am a simple old man who says there are some things that should be left alone, where the game is between the fish and the angler and no reward is given or taken—a place where the odds are generally in favor of the quarry. That's the fair way, the true sportsman's way.

Each day blended into the next as we glided along the glacier-built bays. As the trip was coming to an end, the wind was from the north, and I pointed the canoe toward a blown-down tree so Stuart could make just the right cast. I looked to my right, along a huge slab of granite that had a two-foot depression along its face, where there was a little stream that emptied just up from the depression. I sent my tiny bug just past where I thought a big female bass would be lying in ambush for something that might be brought to her by the flowing water. I twitched the bug slightly and brought it to life. There wasn't a sudden strike, with showers of drops of water going skyward, but my bug just suddenly disappeared from the foamy surface.

I ticked my wrist backward and the fight was on. The smallmouth bass bore deep down, and I could see the brilliant gold and brown colors that set them apart from largemouth bass. She came to the surface and tail-danced around the back of the canoe. *If only my fine line will hold—did I set the hook correctly? Will the hooks hold?* All of these thoughts raced through my head as the aerial display continued.

Slowly, the slight resistance of the willow-like rod took its toll and I could feel the fish's runs getting weaker. I reached down and caught her lip and brought her in. I measured her at 22.5 inches by a chart I carry that says a fish 6 ½ - 7 pounds is about 23 years old. As I took the bait out of her mouth, the rear treble hook fell off into my hand. I gently put her over the side of the canoe, and in a flash she was gone.

Stuart said, "Well, Poppy, looks like you caught the biggest one again."

That was all that was said but it was enough for me.

My wish for you is to always have your canoes pointed in the right direction, may your packs be light, your portages dry and run down hill, and a gently breeze at your back.

Poppy

* * * * *

I always try, during my time on these trips, to slip away by myself. I stick my finger into the water and quickly pull it out. It always confirms my belief that how long it takes the water to fill in where my finger was is just how long I will be remembered after I'm gone. It always tells me how pitiful my efforts really were in the whole scheme of things. When the ripples disappear, there is a real face looking back at me.

    There are no masks that I have so carefully used to cover the face staring back at me so my fellow man cannot see the real me! I always look deep into these eyes that go deep into the water and say these words, "I'll try to do better."

I bid you farewell,
Poppy

The Duck Supper

Dr. Steele Robbins practiced medicine next door to my office for some 40 years. During this time, we became the best of friends. He was a brilliant surgeon and a great outdoorsman.

One Wednesday night, I got a call from Steele stating that he and his wife were going to have a duck supper and that he was about 20 ducks shy of having enough to feed 25 or 30 guests. "I really have my butt in a crack," he said, "and I need you to call for me Friday."

"When's the supper?" I asked.

"Saturday night," he replied.

"Dang, that's not much time," I said, laughing.

Steele answered, "Well, I don't want to put any pressure on you, but you better come through!" He then promptly hung up.

Friday rolled around, and I meet Steele with all my decoys. He had his gun and a little lunch for both of us. We started off in the darkness toward Mayfield Creek bottoms.

Now the mud was about a foot deep and the water was half that amount. Every duck in the world, it seemed, was there. In no time at all, we had all the ducks we needed, and we started home. I had brought a fish stringer and had placed all the ducks on it. Steele said he would pack all the ducks if I would get the guns and decoys. I said okay and as I turned toward the truck, I heard a lone goose call. I proceeded to call him, with my mouth, into range. When he was in shooting range, I went on and added him to our bag. Now 20 ducks and a goose weighed something like 60-70 pounds, but Steele said that was fine, he would carry the stringer.

The weight of the waterfowl began to tire Steele as we were pulling through the mud and muck. All of a sudden, he let out a horrible cry of pain. "Wait, you 'sombitch,' don't leave me!" he cried. He had a charley-horse in the back of his leg. As he nursed himself, I began to filet all those ducks and goose, stuffing the bloody breasts into every pocket of my old hunting coat. When Steele felt that he could go on, we began to move again toward the truck. We had gone maybe 20 yards when he squealed again—this time both legs had charley-horses in them.

There was a huge old log, covered with pond scum and enough coon shit to fertilize a farm. I got him to lie down on the log, and I took off his waders and pants. I began to massage his birdy-white legs, trying to work out the cramps in them. Finally getting the results we wanted, I now had all the decoys, ducks, guns and Steele hanging on me. It was the longest mile I had ever walked. By the time we reached the truck, I had smelled all that gumbo mud, sweat, bloody ducks and all that coon shit that was caked all over him until I was about half sick from the smell.

I got him back to my office and got an IV in him, along with some potassium in his system. His spasms began to calm down. I looked at him and told him that I hoped no one saw us on that log, with me rubbing his bare legs. Boy, I bet that was a sight!

"Yeah," Steele said, "especially with me letting out all those screams."

This was before the gay community was accepted as it is today.

Saturday night came and went and about 1:00 a.m., Steele called me and said, "Well, the supper was a success. We all got drunk and threw the ducks away and drank the soup for supper." Laughing, he continued, "Just kidding. Everything was great! Thanks for helping."

Every day that I go to my office, I walk a mile to Steele's grave and think about all the great fishing and hunting trips that we had together. His old hunting vest hangs on a nail on my den wall. On the back, it simply says: *To Jerry Mills from Steele Robbins.* Plain and straight as an arrow. A lot like he was. When you lose a colorful character like Steele, your Long Journey loses some of its brilliance.

Poppy

Alex

Uncle Clarence was coming home from the University of Kentucky and had called Mama Mills. He told her he was bringing a basketball player home with him. I was so excited they let me stay up late and see just who the player was. As he came through the doorway, he gently stooped and came into the room. This was a giant of a man—6 feet 7 inches! Now, back when I was a little boy, someone over 6 feet was considered tall.

He was very polite as he met Mama and Daddy Mills and then finally me. He said his name was Alex. He and Uncle Clarence had a bite to eat and then they were off to Cairo to see the night lights. The next evening, about 7:00 o'clock, Uncle Clarence was heading north, but Alex decided to stay home. He wandered into the south room where I slept. At the time, I was reading some comic books and listening to good ol' Delta blues music on the old battery-operated radio.

"Hey, kid, what are you reading?" he asked me.

"Oh, some old comic books," I replied. "Want to read some?"

"Sure," he answered.

We began reading those comic books and listening to blues music for the rest of the night. Alex told me all about his youth, his ball playing, and about his family. He had a famous brother, Lou Groza, who was a famous kicker in professional football.

Somewhere around Thursday night, Alex and I had read all of my comic books. He told me that we were going to town the next day to get some candy and something new to read. Sure enough, Friday morning, Alex borrowed Daddy Mills' car—old Betsy—and we were off to Clinton. I couldn't believe how everyone knew my new-found friend. People would come up and ask him to sign something for him.

We finally made it into Peggy Young's dime store. As we went through the door, the smell of candy hit me right in the face.

"What kind do you like, kid?" Alex asked.

"I like 'em all," I replied, "but the kind we generally get is the corn candy. It's the cheapest."

Peggy came out from behind the candy counter and shook Alex's hand. Alex asked where the comic book section was. Peggy pointed to where a fresh shipment had just arrived. Alex stated that we would get one each of the old and new comic books and a sack of candy. Peggy asked him which kind of candy.

Alex answered, "One of every kind."

Peggy said, "Why, there's over 20 different kinds."

With a smile, Alex told him that would be fine.

Alex reached into his pocket and pulled out a roll of bills that was big enough to "burn a wet mule" and peeled off three new $20 bills. He asked Peggy if that would be enough to cover the bill. Peggy said, with a startled look on his face, that it was more than enough. Then Alex said something that was very strange to me.

He said, "Keep the change."

I was used to waiting to get what was left, even down to the last penny.

When we got home, we read deep into the night and then fell asleep listening to blues music. I had eaten so much candy I could hardly go to sleep.

Saturday came, and Uncle Clarence and Alex left. I was sent back to my mundane life style. I listened to U.K. basketball on the radio at Uncle Clyde's house when they won National Titles back to back. Alex was named College Basketball's Player of the Year in 1949.

One Saturday, as I was going into the picture show in Clinton, a classmate ran up to me. In an excited voice, he said, "You know that big fellow that stayed at your house?"

"Yeah," I said.

"Well, he's on the sports newsreel!"

As I waited for the old black-and-white western—with Tom Mix—I could hardly wait to see Alex. Finally, the sports came on and Alex was being interviewed. He was asked what made him so special. He told them with a big grin that it was good coaching, rest and good food. As he turned to leave, he looked back at the announcer and said with a chuckle, "A little candy and comic books helped a lot."

I had always been a huge fan of U.K., but after Tom Payne came on the scene, and with the loss of Coach Rupp, things have never been the same for me. As for Alex, well, he wasn't really a ball player to me. He was just a young boy in a man's body who was extremely nice to a snot-nosed kid from RR 3, Clinton, Kentucky.

The Hobo Who Wasn't

Even though it was a very warm day, it wasn't all that bad. My granddad and I were digging peanuts and hanging them on a drooping, woven wire fence down by an old pond at our family farm at RR 3, Clinton, Kentucky. I was about nine years old, and my granddad had warned me about eating too many raw peanuts. The warning went something like this: "Those raw 'goobers' will give you a case of 'Johnny Quicksteps'."

As I downed a couple more peanuts as he continued his digging, I saw a figure coming from the back field where the railroad split our farm. As the image drew closer, I announced to anyone within a mile's range, "Somebody's coming!"

When he got close enough for me to make out the features of his face, I could tell he was just a wee little man with a round reddish face. He had blonde hair and a thin little mustache. As he started a conversation with Daddy Mills, I noticed a very distinct accent. He said his name was Scotty Scott and that he hailed all the way from Ireland. He asked if there was any way he might work for a place to stay.

"Well," Daddy Mills said, "I can't pay you anything, but you can bunk in the work shed." He pointed to an old building that pumped our water and doubled as storage for grain at one time.

I managed to slip a few more peanuts in while they continued talking. Daddy Mills caught me out of the corner of his eye and said, "I warned you about eating those green peanuts."

With that being said, Scotty walked over and looked at me and said, "Boy, those raw peanuts will give you a good case of the drizzling shits."

Well, it was an instant liking on my part. I thought he was the greatest thing to ever come down the pike! After we got Scotty settled in to where he was going to stay, we pulled out a couple of old tarps for a bed and an old bench to sit on. Scotty seemed as happy as he could be with his new accommodations, as meager as they were.

That fall, Scotty always seemed to be around. About the time the school bus made its way to our house, he always had some stew cooking or a rabbit on a long stick hanging over what he called a slow fire. I was getting better at understanding his accent. For hours he would tell of his adventures in different parts of America. He told about the depression, about his job in a big bank, and about all the banks going "tits up." He told stories about great wealth, lavish parties and men smoking $100 cigars!

Now all of his stories intrigued me a great deal, but it was a different world from mine that he talked about. He told all kinds of long-winded tales about people in New York City and how some of them just could not accept going from riches to rags. He recounted how especially hard it was for some of the people he knew and how they reacted to the "Great Crash." I had heard Daddy Mills talk many, many times of these things. I knew they were true even though I hadn't been very far from our 80-acre farm.

I remember Daddy Mills, Scotty and myself going to the Springhill store to get a loaf of bread. Scotty was getting a can of Prince Albert tobacco when a man in the rear of the store spoke in Daddy Mills' direction and said, "Well, Albert, I see you still got your hobo hanging around."

"His name is Scotty," Daddy Mills said and kept on walking out the door.

Scotty said nothing all the way home. After we reached home and started putting the wagon and team of mules up for the night, Scotty asked if he could borrow the team to go to Clinton and get two trunks that had his belongings in them. The next morning, bright and early, we were at the train station looking at two huge black trunks that were sitting on the side of the old station. On our way home, Scotty told me a story about a man who had left Ireland to make his mark on the world. As things began to go wrong with the economy, the young man caught a freight train and just kept on going.

"Quite a story, don't you think?" Scotty asked. "Promise me one thing, laddie. If you ever travel to Ireland and see Galway Bay, say ol' Scotty said hello. Promise."

"Why, sure, Scotty," I replied, not knowing which way to even start looking for Ireland, much less Galway Bay.

Time passes and seasons come and go. It's early in August as I make my way to the porch to take a sunrise leak. I looked out toward the garden which was probably 30 yards away. There stood ol' Scotty, leaning on his worn out hoe, watching the sun come up.

"Got her all bucked out," he said looking toward me (meaning he had finished hoeing the garden's weeds).

"Looks good to me," I answered. "Got it done 'fore it got too hot, huh?"

"That's right, laddie," was Scotty's response. "Say, by the way, I want you to have my hoe, in case something should happen. You've always had a keen eye on it. In case, you see, I might move on."

"Huh, you're not going anywhere," I said, laughing. "Those trunks are too heavy."

Little did I know. The next morning, Scotty was gone. He left me the hoe, just like he said, on top of the trunks. There was a note, written in beautiful Old English handwriting telling me goodbye and to be sure to visit Ireland someday.

Years passed, and the trunks stayed put, even though I asked my grandparents to please let me look inside them. They always said, "Oh, no, Scotty is going to come back for them some day, and we told him they would be here for safekeeping." That day never came.

Some 50 years later, I inherited the farm. All the buildings were falling down, and the place—like so many old farmsteads around this part of the country—had really gone down. The bulldozer operator, who was tearing down the old buildings, motioned for me to come over and talk. He said that there were a couple of old trunks in the old shed that I might want to look inside to see if I wanted anything out of them. I had forgotten they were there; after all, it had been 45 years since I had seen them.

After I dusted off the tops of the trunks, I pried open the lids and looked inside. I was amazed to see pressed white shirts, fine linen suits and rows of shiny black shoes. There was a small framed diploma from Brown University Banking School tucked neatly under some silk scarves. As I stood there dumbfounded, the operator stormed through the door and broke the silence.

"Hey, bub, what's your answer? Time's wasting."

"Bury it all," I said sadly. "Bury it all."

I finally made it to beautiful Ireland and to Galway Bay. I softly said out loud, "Scotty says hello."

I never hear a freight train that I don't think of Scotty and those days so long ago. As I look at a huge beam in my kitchen, there hangs Scotty's worn out old hoe. It hangs on two nails along with parts of the bridles of Beck and Kate—Daddy Mills' mules—and the latch to the corn crib door. Not much to show for my youth, but I wouldn't trade that old hoe for the best new one made. Because, after all, it was given to me so long ago by the hobo who wasn't.

Poppy

Squirt

There are a lot of good things that happen to us all on our journey through life. One of those things, at least for me, was all the dogs I have owned.

I must have had at least 100 dogs in my time. All of them were very dear to me. However, there was one very special one that came along when I was in my 50's. This story is about this fine specimen of a unique breed.

We lived way out in the country. The closest neighbor was maybe 2.5 miles away, and they didn't have any dogs. At that time, I owned a female Lab named Suzie. Her "season" would come and go with little or no concern, due to no exposure to any male dogs.

On rare occasions, I would hear a coyote or two howling in the night. I paid them no mind, as they seemed to be at a distance.

One cold November day, I was getting some wood to make a fire in our fireplace and Suzie came up for some patting and playful retrieving. She wasn't the greatest retriever, but she was better at it than I was as a teacher. The wind was blowing, but as it would die down, I thought I could hear a puppy whining. I dismissed it as being a squeaky hinge on the shed door.

A few days passed, and as I went back to the woodpile, I heard the whining again. It was then that I spied him sitting, leaning against the edge of the south wall of the shed. The sun was warming that part of the wall. He looked like a little black baseball with hair. I walked over and picked him up and said, "Well, where did you come from?" I was fully expecting to see a whole litter of puppies come out from under the shed, but he was the only one.

Suzie appeared and began licking the pup. "Well," I said, "looks like you've been a naughty girl." I wondered who the daddy was, as I had not seen another dog on the place, and the nearest black Lab must have been at least 10 miles away.

Puzzled, I called my wife and immediately we both fell in love with the little ball of black fur. "Where did it come from?" she asked.

"From Suzie," I replied.

"Who's the daddy?"

I told her I didn't know but that he was the only one.

"Oh," she said, "he's so little."

"Yeah," I answered, "he's just a little squirt."

She suggested that we give him the name Squirt.

"Squirt it is," I said. "Now wait a minute. We don't need another."

"Why not?" my wife asked.

"'Cause," I answered, "we don't need him."

I lost the argument right then and there. His little nose was short and, like I said, he looked like a little black ball of fur. After a few weeks, all that would change. His nose grew long and skinny. His legs grew long with dew claws that ran halfway up his legs. He had beady black eyes, and his tail grew bushy. You know, if I didn't know better, he looked like a black fox or maybe, it hit me, a coyote. It didn't take long for the puppy look to disappear and probably the ugliest varmint you ever saw appeared.

My boys and wife soon lost interest in the pup, so he latched onto me as his sole buddy. As he grew older, his appearance grew worse. Most folks would say that they believed he was the ugliest dog they had ever seen.

"Well, that's not exactly correct," I would tell them. "I believe he's what you call a coydog." A coydog is a cross between a coyote and a dog.

When I would pitch a duck dummy for Suzie, old Squirt would beat her every time. As summer rolled around, he learned to jump up and ride on the fender of my old tractor. All through that summer, he and I must have mowed 1500 acres of pasture. He became the best mouse and rat killer known to man. By his second year, Squirt could kill a copperhead better than any dog I had ever owned.

I took Squirt to Canada for duck and goose hunting many times. His only drawback was that he was so small he had to drag the geese. His mouth was so small he couldn't pick a goose up, so he would straddle them and grab them by the neck and away he would go.

Jim Brummel asked me to go pheasant hunting. He told me to bring a dog if I had one that would retrieve. Well, it had so happened that fall old Squirt had killed a giant copperhead. In the process, the snake had bitten him just above his right eye, and he had a tough time recovering from the bite. I decided to take him on the trip anyway.

Brummel took one look at Squirt and said, "That ugly SOB isn't riding in the cab of my truck. You'll have to put him in that cage on the back of the trailer."

By the time we got to South Dakota to hunt, Squirt looked pretty rough. When the hunt began, there was a M.D. from Minnesota who was called The Colonel. He had decided to grace us with his Yankee Presence. He was a field trial dude who did not lack for confidence. He was dressed as if he had just stepped out of an LL Bean store. He had a boom-boom voice that rang through the countryside like a bull horn. Someone shot a pheasant, and The Colonel told the gallery of hunters just how great his dog was. He then proceeded to tell us he would take the time to show us the fine points of retrieving—Field Trial Style, of course.

The crippled pheasant chose to fly out across a 100-acre field. It was bordered on three sides by Milo that went on forever. It was a picture-perfect stage for The Colonel's fine dog to strut his stuff.

Before the dog started the retrieve, The Colonel explained to us the command to be given and gave a demonstration of the whistle that would be used. He also told us the pedigree of his dog that sounded like something from royalty—"Sir" this and "Sir that."

Well, finally The Colonel lined the dog up and gave the command, and the dog was off. After he had traveled no more than 50 yards, The Colonel blew his whistle. The dog stopped, whirled around and waited for the next command. This went on for some time until something inside of me grew tired of this show. So I just said to old Squirt, who was standing next to me, "Dead bird."

Now I don't know how many folks have ever seen a coyote run across a field. They have sort of a long lope or gallop as they run. Squirt went by "Sir Whacha'-ma-call-it" like a bullet. He was soon at the stand of Milo. He disappeared for a moment and then reappeared with the pheasant in his mouth. Squirt made a straight line for me. As he went by the Lab, I swear he looked at that Lab and seemed to say, "Is this what you're looking for?"

Whenever a pheasant couldn't be found the rest of the hunt, the hunters would be calling for Squirt from all over the field. Finally, The Colonel couldn't find his kill. The bird had fallen right smack dab in the middle of a briar patch and "Sir Do-Haggy" would not go in after it. Squirt jumped up, went in, and instead of taking the bird to me, he just dropped the bird at The Colonel's feet. Lost for words for a few minutes, The Colonel finally spoke. "Your animal does okay here, but he couldn't cut it in my world."

"Well," I said, "that's okay, because we're not in your world today, are we? By the way, how do those little rubber dummies taste?"

The Colonel quickly made his exit.

On the way home, Squirt rode all the way perched up between Brummel and me in the front seat of the truck.

When Squirt was around 13 years old, the family was in the front yard. He was sleeping under one of the vehicles. One of my sons accidentally drove over Squirt. He died in my arms, not 30 yards from where he was born.

Down through the years, you gain some things and you lose some things. This was a great loss for me. Squirt was one-of-a-kind, and he just couldn't be replaced. Every once in a while, I see a coyote watching me mow, and I know they are hated by mankind. But I just can't bring myself to kill one. They don't seem to bother me, so I leave them alone.

I guess the good Lord knows our long journeys, and he occasionally sends us a dog that waits at home for us and loves us whether we're good or bad. Thanks for Ol' Squirt!

Poppy

Papa's Cold North Wind

As they paddled the small johnboat toward the duck blind that was nestled between two cypress trees, they looked at the blind, remembering all their hard work that had taken place.

The blind was a work of art. They had worked and reworked it many times over the past 28 years that they had owned the land it sat on. It fit the surroundings so well that you could barely tell it was even there because it was so cleverly concealed. The old man was nearly 70 now, and his son was 49 years old. They had been hunting partners for so many years that they had lost count. They would go through the same ritual each year by going to the blind a week before duck season opened. They would stock the blind with charcoal, salt and pepper, spices and cooking gear.

After the last decoys were set, they climbed into the blind and began putting coke bottles through a trap door in the floor. A sunken cooler lay beneath the blind in about a foot of cold water.

"Boy, they will taste good next week. Cokes always taste better out of a glass bottle rather than can, don't you think, son?"

"Yes, sir, they sure do," replied his son, "along with a slice of country ham, with two eggs cooked in the ham grease."

They had the same thing for so many years now it was just second nature.

"Papa, how did the ham smell you just had sliced?"

"Great!" Papa said, grinning. "It just doesn't seem like it's been a year since we put those hams down, does it?"

The son shook his head in agreement.

Ducks were coming and going around the small blind. "Wow," the old man said, "Let's sit here a minute and enjoy the scenery."

"Hey, you okay, Papa?"

"Sure, just need to catch my breath a minute . . .all the excitement, I guess."

They sat there for a while and enjoyed the ducks and talked about last year's hunts. After a bit of remembering, they decided to leave for home.

As they reached the truck, which was sitting on a small rise overlooking the swamp, the old fellow said in low, weak voice, "The bank thought I had lost my mind when I bought this 500 acres, but it was the best thing I ever did."

About that time, a brisk north wind came up. The old man, facing the north, said, "Nothing like a cold north wind to stir the innards of an old duck hunter."

That was the last time the old fellow would ever see his beloved swamp. The next morning, he died of a massive heart attack. A few days after the funeral, the first day of duck hunting season rolled around. Even though his heart wasn't in it, the son went through the time-honored ritual of going to the smokehouse, getting the ham, going to the chicken house to get the eggs, then driving to the swamp. Somehow, he felt almost compelled to do this, almost like he had been given an order. He felt himself drawn to the blind.

He parked his papa's old pickup near the rise where they always parked. He opened the door expecting some kind of wind. Instead, there was an almost eerie calm. *Funny*, he thought, I *never remember there not being some kind of breeze.* He went on about his business of getting ready to hunt. He had almost been in a daze for several days since the funeral, with all the confusion that always follows such a loss.

Nearing the swamp, he realized that it was alive with mallards. A huge roar of wings erupted as he pushed the boat from the bank toward the blind. The blind was hidden somewhere in the darkness beyond. He glided by the decoys he and Papa had set out just a few days ago. A feeling of great emptiness came over him. Very soon, he was at the door of the little blind. He stepped inside; it was just like they had left it only days before.

He opened the sack of charcoal and placed a dozen or so brickets in the old charcoal bucket. He lit one small broken piece with a match he found somewhere in his old hunting jumper. Now the inside of the old weather-beaten blind was revealed by a yellowish warm glow from the charcoal bucket.

He placed the sack containing the eggs and ham on the bench beside him. He sat and rested from the short paddle he had made to the blind. As he rested, he thought about how quiet and still it was. There was no wind. *Ducks will come from any direction today*, he thought.

Soon the fire grew red in color and once again the blind was plunged into darkness. As he sat there alone in the darkness, he realized that for the first time in his life, he would be hunting ducks by himself. No one to say, "Hey, good shot!" "How's the ham and eggs?" "Remember that cold morning we turned the boat over getting into the blind?" All those things they had talked about all those years was lost now, he thought.

Many years ago, he and Papa had made a pact to only shoot drake mallards, and only two apiece. Papa had thought four was abusing the law, so two it always was. Also, any duck that had a band on when it was killed, the band was placed in a special drawer. A story was written about the day, and any special memory was placed in a log book, also stored in the drawer. The log book was called The Memory Book.

After 30 minutes or so, light began showing in the eastern sky and soon there was an explosion of light. As shooting time was near, he could hear gun shots all up and down the bottoms. Ducks were coming by the droves, near the pothole where he was set up. He called a soft four-note call as five mallards pitched toward his decoy spread. Two shots and two fat mallard drakes lay on their backs, with their feet paddling wildly in the air. Their head colors showed with the iridescent green, with tiny droplets of water on their breasts glistening in the sun. For a brief second, he almost said out loud, "How about that," but caught himself at the last minute.

He placed an old iron skillet on the charcoal bucket and began to fry a big piece of country ham. Soon the smell of the ham filled the inside of the blind. He then said out loud, "You were right, Papa, it's the best ham we've ever cured." He placed the piece of ham on a plastic plate and began to fry the two eggs. He peppered them and shook a drop of Tiger Sauce over them and let them cook a little while.

He reached down and pulled out a frosty bottle of Coke. He took down a bottle flip that was hanging on a nail, flipped the cap off, and took a big swig. The drink was so cold it nearly took his breath. "Papa, you were right. Cokes are just better out of bottles."

He ate his breakfast at first light. Soon the ducks filled the sky around the little blind. They were settling around him, with all the sounds from whistling wings to soft calls.

It was a defining time in his life, as he sat there for hours, reflecting on the past and wondering about the future. All day there had been no wind. A strange day, he thought. Somewhere, way off in the distance, he heard muffled voices. He took an old pair of binoculars that had belonged to Papa out of its case. He focused them on a new blind on down the bottoms. There seemed to be five hunters, popping their heads up and down, looking in every direction. They disappeared as he heard the sound of geese coming directly toward their blind.

The flock of geese was the same ones that had raised a clutch of young on Papa's and his pothole. They had vowed never to shoot or disturb them in any way. Soon the geese were over the blind, approximately 100 yards high, just out of proper shooting range. He saw five gun barrels emerge, and the hunters emptied all their shells into the flock. One of the young geese shuddered and slowly began to lose altitude and drop out of formation. The men whooped and "high-fived" with a loud noise of laughter.

The geese made their way to the pothole, where he was in full view of them. They set their wings and made a soft landing right in front of his blind. The straggler fought to stay airborne and barely cleared the cypress trees as it made an awkward landing.

His head lay on the water in a clumsy position—he was dying. As he turned on his side, just under his wing a red blotch of blood oozed out of the gunshot hole. Soon he lay his head down in the water and died.

The geese swam and circled around and nudged the dead young goose. As if some silent signal was given, all of the geese rose and circled the blind. They then headed toward the Ballard Refuge. The old goose called helplessly toward her young but to no avail. The geese were soon out of sight.

The sun was slowly setting in the southwestern sky, so the son waded toward the dead goose. He noticed it had a band on its leg. He would take the band's number and enter it into the logbook journal. He would write something about the hunt and place the band in the drawer with all of his and Papa's bands and duck calls.

As he neared the top of the rise, he looked back toward the blind. Ducks were pouring into the swamp by the hundreds, knowing they would be safe for the night. Looking longingly at the blind, he knew what he would write in the journal. *First hunt without Papa*, he thought. He spoke softly out loud, "Wish you could have been here, Papa."

Suddenly, there was a huge blast of north wind that came and went so fast it barely rustled the leaves in the big oak tree near his truck. He spoke again and said, "See you here tomorrow, Papa." Then he left for home.

It is now 20 years later. The son and his 10-year old grandson arrived on opening day of duck season. They had gathered the eggs, cut a new ham and supplied the blind just like he and Papa had done so many times before. The little boy also called him Papa.

They cooked breakfast that morning. The little fellow stated it was the best one he had ever eaten. It was one of these quiet and windless days. All of a sudden, duck sounds could be heard a long way off.

The limit on ducks was still two ducks apiece, just like the limit he and his papa had set so long ago. Of course, it didn't take long for that limit to be filled. This left quite some time for many stories and many questions from the young boy.

"How many acres of swamp do we own, Papa?"

"Oh, 12- or 13 hundred, I suppose," the man replied. "I've picked up maybe 800 or so since my papa died. Maybe you can add some more someday. Anyway, it will all be yours someday soon."

He told the boy that the best land lay to the west where the so-called "takers" used to hunt. He had bought the property about 15 years ago. He told the lad that now the geese could raise their young and never be shot.

He smiled and scuffed the lad's hair. He reached down and opened the trap door, flipped a Coke and handed it to the boy.

"That's so cold it hurts my throat," the smiling boy said. "You know, Papa, I was looking at one of your hunting magazines the other day. I saw a man who had a whole bunch of duck bands on his lanyard that held his duck call. If I ever get one, I think that's what I'll do. How come you don't do that, Papa?"

"Well, it's like this . . . some folks do what you just said to show people what good duck hunters they are. My papa and I would enter the number of the band in our hunting logbook, and then we would write a description of what went on that day. It was sort of a memory reminder to us. I have maybe close to 75 bands in a drawer where I keep mine and Papa's calls."

The boy perked up and said, "Listen, Papa, I hear geese."

Sure enough, they were coming home to roost. There were maybe 400 geese that were raised there and came back to roost every night. Twenty years ago, there were only 11.

"A bunch of game wardens came in here last summer and put bands on a lot of young geese. That was quite a show."

Taking his binoculars out of the case, he focused them for the boy to watch the geese getting closer to the old blind. They flew over the remains of an old blind that looked like a rotting skeleton. It was the same blind where, 20 years ago, the hunters had shot that young goose.

The boy said, "There's one lone goose limping along, Papa."

"Yeah, I see him."

He was struggling to stay airborne, trying his best to make it home to the pothole. Barely clearing the cypress trees, it set its wings and glided onto the water. Badly shot, the young goose lay on his side and finally died.

Watching the boy, the man wondered what his reaction to the whole episode would be.

"Papa, that wasn't a pretty sight."

"No, it wasn't."

"Whoever shot him didn't do a good job, did they?"

"No, but we all mess up sometime."

"Well, I guess so but it's sad to see them suffer. Let's go get him, Papa."

"Well, it's time to go anyway. Get your two ducks and we'll see this old blind tomorrow morning."

"As the boat neared the dead goose, the boy saw the band on its leg."

"Papa, it's got a band!"

"Well, you got a band and didn't have to fire a shot. That's great shooting, if I do say so."

The boy laughed as he lifted the young goose onto the boat.

"Well, what are you going to do with the band?" the man asked. "Put it on your lanyard?"

The boy thought for a moment and said, "No, Papa, I'm going to put it in your drawer with all your bands."

The old man asked the boy what he was going to write in the log book. He had barely gotten the question out when the boy's reply was, "My first duck hunt with Papa."

The boy put his gun, ducks and goose into the back of the old pickup truck. The old man looked back at the swamp where hundreds of ducks and geese were pouring into the spread for a restful night. The boy said, "Quite a sight, huh, Papa?"

Suddenly, a cold north wind briefly blew a harsh blast of cold air into their faces. "Wow, did you feel that, Papa?"

"Yeah, son, that happens quite often here. I'll tell you about that on the way home."

The boy got in the truck and shut the door. The old man turns back toward the swamp again and simply says, "See you tomorrow, Papa."

Perhaps when the young boy grows up, someday he will bring his boy to the blind. Perhaps there will be two separate winds from the north—one to say "Good morning" and one to say "Good night." It seems long journeys must end so others can begin.

Poppy

Dreams of Home

I've always tried to take the time to talk with my patients. Invariably, I'll ask them, "Where's home?" They generally answer by asking, "Where I live now or where is my real home?" "Real home," I reply.

They start by saying that when they were kids, home was someplace in a different time than the present. I ask what makes them think of home. They usually say, "Oh, sounds, smells, special events, and people who remind me of someone back then." That is the same with me.

I now call home a small three-room cabin nestled deep in a big woods. It is not small by chance but small by choice. We heat with wood in a wood stove or a fireplace . . .again not by chance but by choice.

The other night as I put a stick of stove wood in the little stove, there was the visual puff of smoke that came out as I closed the door. "Hmm," I said to my wife, "that hickory smells great!" I spit, as always, on top of the stove and watched it bounce all over the stove, finally disappearing.

She spoke very softly at first and asked, "Why do you do that?"

"Guess it's just the little boy in me. I did that when I was at home."

"I suppose you peed off the front porch, too, like you do now."

"Yeah," I said, going back to that hickory smell.

"You're dreaming about home again, aren't you?"

"Guess I was."

"I've noticed certain smells, sounds or something from the past seems to trigger these dreams."

"Uh, huh."

"Well, I got some time, tell me about home."

Now as if I hadn't told her a million times, I thought a million and one wouldn't hurt.

"Well, home to me was a time between 1941 and 1948. The smell of hickory smoke reminded me of winter when we burned wood at hog killing time. We had to have a smoky fire to cure the bacon and hams. Also, we had to boil water to wash our clothes. You know, I would take a bath once a week in the blueing wash water in a #3 wash tub, whether I needed it or not. That was it for that week.

I can still smell Featherston's Store at Springhill. Do you remember what laying mash, a blacksmith shop, or Baco's chicken hatchery smelled like?"

"No," she replied.

"How about 200 baby chickens in those big pasteboard boxes, with the little round holes on the side?"

"No," she answered again, "but go on."

"When I was little, I played games by myself. One was to see how many horseflies I could kill with the plow line on old Beck's and Kate's butts. Say, did you ever put a chicken feather up a horsefly's butt and see how far it could fly?"

"No," she said. "Now get back about home."

"Okay. Sounds remind me a lot about home . . .like the way a bucket sounded, hitting the water deep down in a cistern. The way a mule chomped on an ear of corn. Maybe the way six half-grown kittens drank when I milked our cow and trained a squirt of milk in their direction, just to watch them fight for every drop.

"Voices from the past are always a reminder of home. I can still hear those voices even though they have been gone many years. Special times were few but nevertheless important. I remember the annual trip to Paducah to see the fair. We also visited with Mama Mills' brother, a surgeon and Chief of Staff at old Riverside Hospital. His office was in the tallest building in Paducah. I can still remember the man who operated the elevator. He was dressed in his uniform with all the shiny buttons and his pillbox hat. He always said, 'Which floor, please and watch your step.'

"After the visit with the doctor, it was off to Kreskey's to eat my once-a-year chicken salad sandwich on toast. Funny how that was such a memory about home.

"Then there was decoration day. You remember when all the graves had fresh-cut flowers placed on them. This was the time before impersonal plastic ones.

"I remember Christmas when we were all home. I remember the sights, sounds and smells of steam engines and later trains with names like the City of New Orleans, City of Miami and the Panama Limited. I watched people sitting, reading and even eating as they briefly entered my small world and, in a blink of the eye, they were gone. I suppose all old creosoted timbers that a make a trestle and ties, along with our old slough, smelled the same. But I didn't know about them—only the one behind our house.

"I found myself, on many occasions, looking up and down those tracks, wondering what was at the end.

"I recall that old mail plane that flew from Chicago to Memphis. It flew directly over our farm. I wondered if it ever landed."

I hadn't noticed that my wife had left the room but had just kept talking like she was still there. The fire was getting low so I stepped outside to get some wood. I looked up at the cold, star-studded sky. I said out loud, "They're all gone now—the house, the barn, all the out-buildings. All my family I knew as a boy have gone. Home is gone, never to reappear—only as a dream."

My wife came out on the porch and asked, "You're not going to pee off the porch, are you?"

I smiled and said, "I can't seem to please you, so I decided to get down on the ground and pee up on the porch . . .see if you liked that better."

We both laughed and went inside and banked the coals up for the night.

Where once stood a young boy dreaming of his future, now stands an old man who found out where the tracks ended and the planes land. He now knows home is neither a place or time. It's now an emotion. He dreams not of the future now but only of the past, his favorite dream being Dreams of Home.

I bid you farewell,
Poppy

Dab

It was the year of 1962 and I had just finished my sophomore year at the University of Louisville Dental School. I had ended my E.R. and oral surgery rounds at General Hospital, and my butt was really dragging.

I had to have a summer job. My only choice was working for the Graves County School Board of Education, doing clean-up for all the county schools. On Monday morning, I was standing in front of "The Boss," getting my orders for the day. He looked up from reading the sports page of *The Courier Journal* and said, "Doc, you go with that fellow over there, to the Water Valley school and paint the johns." That was all he said and then gracefully strolled out the door.

My co-worker reminded me of the colorful character in the song *Mr. Bojangles*. He was sort of unkempt, if you know what I mean. He seemed plastered to the wall like a fly that had escaped the first frost of the year, waiting for the inevitable to come. His eyes were bloodshot and his hair had not been brushed. He had all the characteristics of most of the folks I had been treating at General Hospital . . . you know, that look of despair.

"Hi, I'm Dab. I paint and drink a wee bit," he said.

I soon learned that a "wee bit" took on a whole new meaning for me.

"I guess you can just call me Doc," I replied as we made our way to the old schoolhouse in Water Valley.

I kept seeing him reach beneath the seat of the old pick-up truck we were in. He would turn and look out the window, take a quick swig, and then place the bottle back under the seat. Now, it's about 18-20 miles to the school, so Dab was well on his way by the time we got there.

We got all the paint, brushes and drop cloths out. Next, we soon opened the "john" doors to one of the worst smells I think I ever smelled. No one had flushed the toilets before leaving for summer break, and the doors were shut. With the summer heat and the smell of all that urine, mixed with the smell of Kemtone Sea Spray green paint, it wasn't long before I was about half sick. By this time, Dab was "drunker than a skunk."

The time was the beginning of the Vietnam war. The troop build-up was just starting. The troop planes, from Fort Campbell, were practicing drops. They would make their turns right over the schoolhouse we were painting. I was painting the wall where the only window was. There was a broken glass pane in the window right above me. As the plane flew over, really low, it shook out a sliver of glass that came down and struck me in the arm and stuck there.

It seemed to me that I had sewed up half the population of Louisville at General Hospital. I had also seen many buckets of blood but not mine. It was squirting out everywhere.

Dab asked, "What's wrong?"

When I turned to say something, Dab saw the glass sticking in my arm with blood squirting out. To this day, I can still remember him saying, "It's getting a little warm in here." About this time, Dab hit the floor.

I took my belt off and cinched it around my arm, grabbed the glass and pulled it out. When I did that, blood squirted everywhere. Old Dab had a big safety pin holding up his overalls. I got the pin and pinned it into my arm. When I pulled up on the pin, I could cut off the blood to some extent. I had a string in my pocket so I tied it to the safety pin. I then put the string in my mouth and tugged on the other end.

I got Dab propped up and got some ice from my drinking cooler. I then put the ice in a rag and tied it around Dab's head. He had a big knot on the back of his head. He was just coming to as I reached the door.

"Hey, Doc, could you bring me a bottle from under the seat . . .maybe two bottles?"

By the time I got back with the bottles, I was getting pretty weak from all the blood loss. As I hit the door coming back to the room, the smell of the stale urine, the scent of the paint, and the smell of the booze from Dab was about all I could take.

"Be back soon, Dab," I called out. "Just stay put."

My Uncle Clarence practiced medicine in Clinton, which was only 15 miles away, so down the road I went in that old truck. I had the string in my mouth, tugging as hard as I could, trying to stop the blood from squirting. By the time I got to Clinton, the inside of the truck's cab looked like I had chopped off a chicken's head. Blood was everywhere.

"Unk" sewed me up, gave me a tetanus shot and a big slug of cold penicillin in my butt. As I drove back to the school, I noticed the bandage on my arm was full of blood. I was dripping a little bit, but that could be expected. I figured I would change it when I picked up Dab to go home.

Ol' Dab was just finishing the last bottle when I walked in. He saw the bloody bandage. "Getting warm in here again," he said. Out he went, but this time he fell face forward. It sounded like you might have dropped a pumpkin from a two-storied window, with a smacking sound.

I rolled him over and a knot jumped up between his eyes that matched the one on the back of his head. This time, the worst damage was to his nose, which now pointed toward his right ear. I finally got his nose back somewhere in the middle of his face. Then I dragged him to the truck. Ol' Dab was too drunk to feel much pain and he could hardly talk.

"Could you take me home?"

"You sure you're going to be alright?"

"Yeah," he said, looking in the mirror. "Nice job on my nose, Doc. Last time that happened it cost me $128 to get it set."

As I drove Dab home, he asked me where I lived. I told him I was staying at my mom's and dad's house for the summer at 817 So. Pryor St. "Oh," was all he said. He told me he lived over by Black Humphrey's Tobacco Warehouse. He said that I could let him off at the Vet's office and he would walk the rest of the way. I told him I didn't think that was a good idea because he was so banged up from all his falls.

We drove by an overgrown vacant lot. Dab mentioned that this was it, and he disappeared into the weed-infested lot. I eased along behind him a safe distance away. There it was—a shack of tin and old planks. I returned to the truck unnoticed.

All the rest of the summer, we talked about far-away places, about things he had never seen or even dreamed about. Dab always wished he could go to some of these places. He would get a far off look in his eyes and said he guessed he never would.

"Shoot," I told him, "you've got a railroad track about 100 yards away. Just think of an empty boxcar as your own private train!" I laughed at myself for even saying that.

I still believe that was the longest, hottest summer I can ever remember. As Dab and I lined up for our final jobs, the "Boss Man" told us to go to Hickory and paint the outdoor john for the Negro school there. I did not know that they didn't go to the public schools.

I was told that there were five such schools in the county. "Just get the job done," he said.

Dab and I found this one-room schoolhouse on a small lot that was grown up in weeds. The outside of the school had been needing paint for a long time. There was an old tire hanging from a nearby tree. That was the only playground equipment. Sure enough, there was an outdoor john sitting behind the school.

As I stepped into a small foyer of the school, I couldn't believe my eyes. There was a hot plate, a can opener, a pair of old pliers, and seven spoons with the handles painted different colors. An old barrel served as a trash can and was full of empty pork and beans cans. Six cans of pork and beans neatly sat on the shelf with the hot plate.

"Can you believe this, Dab?"

He never said a word.

"All they had to eat was pork and beans?" I questioned.

"I guess so," was all Dab would say.

The teacher apparently would open a can and put it on the hot plate. Then, when the can got hot, she would take the pliers to pick up and hold the can and give it to a student.

"This is hard to believe," I said.

"Look here, Doc, they've got a bunch of old books, no chalkboard and a few worn-out desks," Dab answered.

"We've got to do something about this," I replied.

"What can we do," asked Dab. "We don't have any books or food."

I reached in my pocket and fumbled around for the master keys to all the schools in Graves County. "Yeah, but we've got these!"

Next summer came around, and I went to visit old Dab. The lot had been cleaned up—no weeds, no shack, no Dab. I went to the maintenance building to see if anyone knew anything about Dab. The man in charge said that he didn't know where Dab was. He told me that Dab had left about the same time I had left for school. No one had seen hide nor hair of him since then. He then told me he knew that Dab had quit drinking. However, he told me he had heard a rumor.

"What rumor?" I asked.

The man said it seemed that someone had put a new blackboard, seven new desks, all kinds of new books, and enough canned goods to feed an army at the Hickory schoolhouse. But the kicker . . .they had left a two-burner cook stove that said "donated by D&D School Supplies."

"I guess you wouldn't know anything about all that, would you, Doc?" inquired the man. "Also, did I mentioned a new paint job on the inside?"

"Well, you know about rumors. They are kind of like the wind blowing," I said as I ambled out the door.

When I got to my mom's home, she told me she had forgotten to tell me I had gotten the strangest card. About a month ago, a card had come that had a picture of New Orleans, Jackson Square. It was addressed simply to "Doc, 817 So. Pryor St., Mayfield, KY." On the other side was only one word—Dab.

There now sits that one-room schoolhouse on the campus of Graves County High School. The building is being renovated to show folks, I guess, how far we've come. However, this school was being used by black children 30 years after all the other communities had new schools for white children.

Somewhere in all of us there is a part that knows what is fair and a level playing field. It is a shame that this went on right under our noses for so long. Someone in power at the time condoned and supervised this terrible act against those kids. Just think what it would be like to have your kids have only a can of beans for dinner every day.

I went inside that building the other day and thought to myself, *I don't care how many coats of paint they apply to the walls, this crime can't be painted over.*

As Paul Harvey used to say, "Now you know the rest of the story."

Dab & Doc School Supplies

The Shoe Shine Boy

This story is about a little farm boy who is moved to a ghetto section of a large city—a place where there was a lady of the night on every street corner. A place where a lot of people wondered where their next meal would come from or where to find a shot of whiskey. Also, where to find a piece of light bread to strain a bottle of liquid shoe polish through for a drink later in the day. Even worse, a heroin fix to tie him through the day. It was a place where the social structure was measured by poverty and despair.

Sometime later, the boy moved to a small town where that social structure changed. Things there were determined by how much money you had or your ancestry. This story begins early one morning, the very first day of school's summer vacation. He would begin the eighth grade the next fall. An announcement was made from the boy's mother, "This is the day to sign up for your Social Security card and find a summer job."

"But Mom, I don't know where to look for a job or what I can do."

"Try the Country Club," she said. "Your dad is thinking about joining, for business reasons."

Soon, he was shining and cleaning off golf shoes in the mornings and caddying in the afternoons at the Club. The summer dragged on until the boy's mother told him that he had done a good job, saving his money to help buy his new school clothes.

"School starts next week," she said, "so why don't you wear your swimming trunks under your clothes and take a good swim in the pool. You've earned it."

After work on that hot August afternoon, the boy jumped into the pool. Immediately, 17 kids got out of the pool. They ran, shouting to the golf pro that the shoeshine boy was in the swimming pool. Some said, "No, it's the caddy." It was like a "horse turd" dropped from the sky and landed in the middle of the pool.

The pro dropped to one knee next to the pool. He wiggled his finger for the boy to approach him. He then asked him if he was the boy who shined and cleaned golf shoes and caddied.

"Yes, sir," the boy replied shyly.

"What's your name, son?" the pro asked. The boy told him his name.

"Hasn't your dad recently joined the Club?"

This time, the answer came in a strong and proud voice, "Yes, sir!"

The pro turned around to the crowd of kids, palms raised and stretched upward as if to calm an angry crowd. He announced in an authoritative voice, "It's okay, kids, he is a member."

The boy immediately got out of the pool as all the kids jumped back in. He left for home. As he began his long walk home, he made himself three promises that day. One, to never shine shoes again for someone too lazy to do it himself. Two, never pack a bag of frivolous toys again. Three, and the most important, never to return to "The Club" again. He would swim, from now on, with the little black boys in the creek that ran close to town.

A lot of time passed and the boy grew to be a man. One day, while shopping at a local grocery, he saw a tattered old man sifting through the assortment of meats, looking for the cheapest buy. He walked over and picked up the most expensive meat in the cooler. He placed it in the old man's cart. He then put a $20 bill on top of the meat.

"What's that for?" the old man asked.

"Oh, you don't remember, but once upon a time, you taught me some very important lessons. I've used them down through my lifetime. I owed you a debt I've never paid until now."

The tattered old man replied, "I'm glad I did something right for a change."

He watched out of the corner of his eye as the old man shuffled toward the cashier. Thinking to himself: *That old man was one of the boys who led the shouting kids to the golf pro.* Then he smiled and mumbled to himself, "Debt paid in full."

Just by chance, you might ask what were those lessons learned so long ago. "What you say and do really does affect others." And last, but certainly not least, is to know the meaning of a word that brings about embarrassment and nauseating pain deep in your gut. That is to be made to feel HUMBLED before your peers. I've known the boy all his life and he's thankful for those lessons learned so long ago.

Poppy (The Shoeshine Boy)

* * * * *

Sometime later, my wife was reading the local paper. She read out loud, "The local Golf and Country Club has gone bankrupt."

My reply was, "Ain't that a daisy!"

The Daisy Church

There had been a huge building program that was finally finished. A large sanctuary and education building had been placed on a 25-acre site along a busy highway. The church leaders had torn down the old church building, citing "business reasons." No one could return, even if they wanted to.

There was an old man and his wife who just didn't feel comfortable in the new church. It was so big with so many new members they felt like they were lost in the shuffle. Finally, they dropped out of church. They had been attending the same church for over 40 years.

After a few Sundays went by, the old couple though that there must be something they could do to help people. There was a void in their lives now. The old man had been a deacon for 40 years. But over the years, he had forgotten the scriptures that were given to him when he took his vows to become a deacon.

The old man called the preacher of the big church to ask him about the scriptures. The preacher's wife said he would call him right back. But no call came. He then called two more preachers from different churches. Still no reply. *Well*, he thought, *I'm glad it didn't concern my salvation*. The old man and woman looked up the scriptures for themselves. The scriptures told of taking care of the widows and children.

The old man was a good fisherman, and his wife was a good cook. They started cooking fish with all the trimmings and began taking meals to shut-ins and widows. On the back of the plates they served the food on, the old woman drew a simple daisy with the saying "Jesus loves you."

Well, it wasn't long before the people that they visited and fed would ask for prayer for themselves and friends. Then they would ask the old couple to send a note or card to a loved one. Before long, the requests were so large that all their spare time was devoted to cooking fish meals and writing cards and letters. Quickly it became a full-time job.

One day, the couple went for a drive in a neighboring county. They drove down a lonely country road that ended in front of a very small church. There was a young man putting the final touches of paint on the building, so the old couple stopped to chat. The young man said he was the new preacher of this very small and poor congregation.

The old man asked, "Who owns that small cabin over there?"

"Oh, it's part of the church's property, but no one lives there anymore," the young man answered.

"Not you?" the man asked.

"No," the preacher replied, "I have my own house. I'm a carpenter so I draw no pay for pastoring here." He continued, "You could probably move in for a small fee. Maybe you could help me mow or help take care of the church, but there would be no pay."

As they drove home, the couple talked about the church and how they might fit in there. To make a long story short, they sold their home and moved to the cabin. There were only 16 people, all retired, who made up the tiny congregation. The church had no electricity, carpets or soft pews. They had an outdoor "privy." There was a fairly large tin-covered shed out back of the church. It was used for dinners on the grounds or a place to cook.

In a very short time, the congregation began cooking meals and sending letters that had daisies, prayers and scriptures on them. All of the members were happier than they could ever remember. Requests starting pouring in from everywhere. Soon, they could barely keep up, but it had become a labor of love. This continued for many years, and finally the old couple passed away.

One spring day, years later, a couple from Mississippi slowly drove up in front of the little church. They were surprised to see 16 folks under the tin shed laughing and having a good time, while cooking fish and preparing meals. Some were busy writing letters. The couple approached the preacher who was replacing a window pane in the front of the church.

They asked him, "What in the world are these folks doing, and what is the name of this church?"

"Well, we go by the name of The Daisy Church, and all these people are busy helping others."

The wife said, "I've never seen that many daisies growing before in my life."

The preacher drew a long breath and replied, "Most of the daisies are around that old cabin. They started spilling over into the church yard about 20 years ago. They cover up about all the yard now. We don't even have to mow anymore. They stay all summer long."

The couple told the preacher that they were looking for a church that was small but very active in helping others. The preacher smiled and asked them what they had done before retiring. They said the wife had cooked in a school for handicapped children and her husband had raised catfish. The preacher told them that the cabin was empty and that they were welcome to it.

As the preacher turned to watch the lady admiring all the daisies, he could almost read her mind. *Over a million daisies now, with more to come*, the preacher thought to himself.

"This is it, John, this is what we've been looking for!" the lady exclaimed.

Long ago, I went to a church like The Daisy Church. It was very small and not wealthy at all. We didn't have indoor plumbing or soft pews. I can remember, as a seven-year-old child, Vernon Peery stepping to the pulpit and announcing that we were going to have a business meeting. The meeting went something like this:

"Who needs prayer?"

My grandmother would always ask prayer for our boys in the service. Someone else would say that a neighbor's barn roof needed repairing and that he needed some help. Then, someone else would tell of a person who was having a hard time.

I know the prayers worked because my uncle and dad came home after the war was over. That barn roof somehow got repaired. The next week after the business meetings, Vernon would get up and read a note, thanking the church for the gift. Now, we didn't have a huge blinking sign in front of our church, or carpets or padded seats. We may not have been The Daisy Church, but we were pretty darn close.

Poppy

The Call Home

Duane Webb was in my office a while back and we were talking about hunting, a subject that I knew a little bit about. Word usage is not one of my better attributes, and as always, I was making more than my share of errors.

I said, "That is the most amazingist thing."

Duane, who is a retired English school teacher, immediately said that there was no such word as "amazingest."

"Well," I said, "my granddaddy said it that way and so did my daddy. So there it is."

"Nope," he said.

I knew my next sentence would tear him up good, but I said it anyway. "Well, if it ain't a word, it orta' be."

With that, Duane just shook his head and muttered these words, "Against stupidity, even the gods battle in vain." He then ambled off toward the front door.

I thought for a minute and remembered Daddy Mills and me trying to fix a downed wire on our local phone line out of Springhill, KY. I'm sure you all know about locust posts. They are just crooked as a snake, but it was all we had. The whole line was strung on those crooked posts. Some were 20 feet tall and some were 10 feet tall. As we looked back at the posts, it looked like some drunk comedians had put them in. They leaned one way and then another.

We then put the glass insulators, courtesy of the Illinois Central Railroad Telegraph (discarded, off course), on the locust posts with some bailing wire. The posts were then put in a hole we had dug with a set of fence post diggers.

As Daddy Mills looked up at the wire after the job was finished, he said out loud, "That's the most amazingest thing I ever did see."

I thought he was talking about the job we had finished. "No, not the job," he said. "How can somebody over around Shiloh call us, night or day, and talk over that wire? It's the most amazingest thing in the world."

I agreed.

We got home around suppertime. Mama Mills read us a letter from Uncle Clarence, their son. He was a paratrooper in Europe during World War II. The letter was quite short, as I recall, only a few sentences. It said that he was safe now and that he might get to come home soon. Well, a month went, and then one day the old phone rang three long rings.

Mama Mills said, "Answer the phone. That's our ring."

I answered the phone and a woman's voice said, "Jerry, boy, this is Anna Lee at the switchboard in Springhill. Go get Miss Estil, There's someone calling long distance."

Mama Mills picked up the phone, and her face turned as white as the baking flour on her hands. Mama Mills began to cry. Daddy Mills was sitting next to the wood stove, listening to Gabriel Heater and the war news. Mama Mills talked for about three minutes. As soon as she hung up, she started telling us that Uncle Clarence was in New York and that he would be home in a few days. She then went to the kitchen and started cooking all his favorite cakes, pies and foods.

I can still remember the look on Daddy Mills' face as he stared at the old wooden telephone that hung on the wall in the middle room. He marveled, "That's the most amazingest thing. Think of the miles of wire his voice traveled through to get to that wood phone box on the wall—all the way from New York!"

Clarence went on to make M.D. and practiced some 40 years. The last day he practiced at home in Clinton, KY, there wasn't much fanfare. He didn't get a key to the city or any fancy awards, just a lot of pats and thanks. You know, Clarence dodging all those bullets, and a country boy becoming an M.D., was quite a feat. But to me, the most amazingest thing was when he called home, so long ago.

Thanks, Chauncy!

I bid you farewell,
Poppy

The Circle

I was in the process of tying some streamer flies out in my cabin one night. As I put on the final touches, I thought about something I had read as a boy. It was how some sportsmen make a complete circle in their pursuit of fish. It generally starts off by fishing for blue gill or pollywogs with a can of worms, a cane pole, a cork, line and hooks. Most of the time, the fish come from some small creek or muddy little pond. That was the way I started my circle, which has taken me some 65 years to complete.

I don't know why I was even tying these flies. I knew I would never return to Alaska to fish that remote river—just a funny habit, I guess. I placed them in a plastic box and wrote on a small slip of paper the time and presentation I used to catch huge Chinook salmon.

I had recently returned from that fast snowy-colored stream and decided I had completed my circle. I resolved I would devote more time to my grandkids' fishing education. My wife Alyce called me to the phone. It was "Snort," now six years old. He was one of my grandsons who possessed the greatest desire to fish.

"Hey, Poppy, how 'bout taking me fishing tomorrow?"
"Okay," I replied. "What do you want to catch?"
"Fish," came the answer.
"Alright, I'll pick you up around eight."
"I'll be ready," he said. "You got me a pole, Poppy?"
"Sure thing," I said. "I'll get it and find some bait."

I thought about the tackle we would use. To myself, I said, "Well, I can't let him use one of my good rods, he can't cast. What will I use?" I looked up in the rafters of the old porch and found there were a couple of old cane poles his daddy had fished with as a boy. "Guess that will have to do."

New lines, corks, and hooks were quickly made up and tied to the old poles. Grabbing a shovel and a tin can, I went to digging worms. Soon I had enough to catch every fish in the pond.

Even though I hadn't fished the pond I had chosen to fish with the boy in some 60 years, I felt confident we would catch a lot of fish. I thought numbers, not size, would be the most important thing.

Well, when we got to the pond, I went to the exact spot that I had fished as a young boy. After a lot of noise and laughter about catching a couple of leopard frogs and crawdads, we settled down to some serious fishing.

The boy caught and I baited. I had never seen fish bite that fast in my life. After a "zillion" tiny brim, I suggested maybe moving over to the side where I knew bigger brim would be. However, he was quite content catching small brim and lots of them. Finally, as we were running low on worms, a snake doctor sat on his cork. I told him a bigger fish would bite soon. No more than the words cleared my mouth, the cork disappeared beneath the surface. A big brim had bit! The kid was all over the pond bank, fighting the fish. The tip of the old pole finally broke and the fish vanished deep in the water.

"Dang, did you see that big brim, Poppy? He was huge! Tomorrow, let's fish over yonder where the big ones live."

"Remember now," I said, "when you leave this spot to catch bigger fish, you are starting your circle."

Totally confused, he couldn't think of anything to say but, "They're so big!"

"Yeah, but harder to catch."

"I don't care. I want to catch big ones."

As we left for home, I thought that he may not come back to that spot for a long time. But when he does, maybe he'll remember I was with him when he started his circle.

As I wrote the events of the day in my journal that night, I thought how neat it was for me to have been there that day. I recorded all that I had seen and heard in my last chapter of my fishing journal.

Many years have passed. I marvel at the fishing strides "Snort" has made. He has caught many fish of different species from fresh to salt water. He has even won a contest while fishing for red fish in the Gulf of Mexico. He has fished in Canada for small-mouth bass, pike, and walleyes. He has many trophies on his walls at home. As I have watched him over the years, he is light years ahead of where I was at the same age.

I have observed over the years that there are some kids who like to fish and some who love to fish. Every once in a while, there is one who was born to fish. As I explained this to my wife, I asked her, "I wonder where he gets it from?"

She just smiled and said, "Yeah, I wonder."

Maybe I'll be around in a few years if his kids want to fish. May as well get started now. I wonder if anyone sells cane poles anymore?

On my long journey, I've noticed how fast things move along in today's times. Fishermen are so far advanced with skills and equipment. However, I wonder if they really take the time to enjoy their circle.

Poppy

Miracles

As he approached my office, I thought to myself, *He's one of those carefree, spirited characters that you can't help but like.* He came into the oral surgery operatory and sat down. He peered over at me, with a twinkle in his eye, and asked, "Seen any miracles lately, Doc?"

"I guess you being here would constitute one," I replied. "I've been after you for five years to get that place on your lip checked out."

"Well, it's time we took care of the little ol' thing, Doc. Tell me the bad news first."

"I don't have any good news. So here's what I do know: When I take it out, it will take 28 days to heal. Your lip will probably be lumpy due to the scar tissue, and your lip may be a little numb."

"Is that all?"

"No, if it is malignant, it could cost you your lip or even your life."

"Well, is that all?"

"No, it's going to hurt like hell. If you had done this five years ago, and not smoked or dipped and stayed out of the sun, your chances would be a lot better."

"Looks like I need one of those miracles you seem to see all the time."

"More than you know, Richard," I said.

"Well, let's get crackin'," he replied with a grin.

The tumor was a little larger and more angry than I had thought. Finally, I got it all, or at least I got all I could see. I completed suturing up the wound. I went back over what he was to expect—pain, a possible numb lip, a lumpy area from scar tissue, and A Big Chance of Cancer.

It didn't phase him in the least. He bounced down the hall and looked back at me. With a cheery tone in his voice, he stated, "I never saw a miracle, but you've seen enough for us both, I guess. So, I'll just wait for mine. See you, Doc." He then promptly left.

I placed the tumor in the specimen bottle. I then thought of my old friend (the pathologist) who would examine it and tell me if it was malignant. For some reason, I felt especially afraid that this one would be bad. So I took a little time to call the University and talk to Tom, the pathologist.

"Hey," he said, "you don't call except when things look bad. Got a tough one, huh?"

"Yeah, I'm worried about this one," I said. "Give me a call as soon as you can, will you?"

"Sure. Hey, remember all those long nights while we were at school?" he asked. "I especially remember those long nights at that old Kroger Warehouse, unloading box cars after school. I remember talking about what a miracle it was for us to get that far along in our education. Me from Slippery Slope, KY and you being from someplace called Spring Hill."

"Yeah, that was quite a miracle, wasn't it? Two hayseeds in the Big City."

"Well, I'll get those results to you in a couple of days. I know you're anxious about this one."

Sure enough, two days rolled around, and I got the call. No malignancy! I thanked him for the rush. Then I breathed a big sigh of relief.

When Richard came back to have the sutures removed, he said, "I thought you said it was going to hurt, be lumpy and numb."

"Well, I thought it would be all those things. By the way, it wasn't cancer."

After he left, I just shook my head. Then I heard him come back through the door. "Think that was my miracle, Doc?" he asked.

"You can bet on it, old buddy," I replied. "I'm glad you finally got to see one!"

Funny, I thought to myself, *I saw at least five or six miracles just on you.*

The very next Sunday, my pastor asked at the close of the service if anyone had seen any miracles that week. A small number of hands went up. The pastor then said, "Let's give thanks for them."

As we bowed our heads in prayer, the pianist began playing *Amazing Grace*. I thought back in time to when I reached over and tugged my grandmother's sleeve and asked her if I could go outside church to visit the outdoor privy. It was one of those August summer nights. There was a revival at Spring Hill Baptist Church. After I had finished my business, I headed back toward the old church. I heard the lady start to play *Amazing Grace*. Now, most of the time, about every third note would stick on that old piano. About every other note was usually wrong. Usually it was difficult to recognize the hymn. But on this occasion, Van Clyburn could not have played it any better. The song leader rarely sang on key, but this time he did. The little choir sang their hearts out.

That night was the very first miracle I remember. It was when a 10-year old kid actually understood the miracle that old song told about.

The miracles were always there. It's just my sight got a lot better the longer my journey continued.

I bid you farewell,
Poppy

Box of Dreams

As I came into the rest home, I had to go by the front desk. The lady sitting there said, in a pleasant voice, "Hey, Doc, I've got a new one in 37."

Thanking her, I went down the dark hallway hearing all the sounds of groaning and coughing coming from each room on corridor C. I had only been on staff there six months or so. Already I sensed the feeling of hopelessness with the 70 or 80 inhabitants. My job description was to help with their oral health and to keep them as comfortable as possible. By this time, many had lost track of time as to what year or day it was. Some were confused as to whether it was day or night.

Every so often, you would run into someone who really shouldn't be there. Such was the case of Lon. As I went into the room, Pete looked up and said, "I guess you've come to meet Lon."

"Yep, I have."

Pete was going to be Lon's roommate for as long as he would be at . . . shall we say, Shady Acres. We'll call it that in place of all the "catchy" names that are given to these types of institutions.

"Hi Lon. I'm known around here as Doc."

"Glad to know you, Doc," he said in a shy quiet voice.

"What's the reason for your stay here, Lon?"

"My sons married, and their wives said that they didn't want me. They've all moved away now, so here I am."

"Mind if I examine your mouth?"

"Okay."

"You look alright. Have any swallowing problems? Any pain?"

"No," Lon replied.

"Says here on your chart you have angina. Taking your nitroglycerin?"

"On occasion, when the need arises."

I stopped writing on the chart. Here was a man, very articulate. He seemed alright, and he could answer questions intelligently. He looked like a piece of driftwood deposited on an uncharted sandbar by a receding river, left to decay in the sun. He seemed confused as to what he could do about the whole thing. All he really needed was loving relatives...someone to come by and check on him and let him live out his days at home.

"Well, Lon," I said, "I see you have an old cheese box. I had one just like that when I was a boy."

After that statement, we would become more than friends. We would become Keepers of the Dreams.

"Hey, Doc, would you like for me to tell you a short story my daddy told me when I was a boy?" Lon asked.

"Sure, Lon. How short is it?"

"One minute and 32 seconds."

I laughed and said, "Got it down to the seconds, huh?"

"Yes, sirree, Doc."

"I'll time you and we'll see how close you come. What's the name of the story?"

"*The Great Marble Shootout.*"

Seems the story took place in the slums surrounding Louisville General Hospital. Many of the residents in the area went for free medical and dental treatment. It had been stated there was more disease in a four-block radius around the Medical and Dental Schools and General Hospital than in any area in the state.

The story opened in the backyard of a run-down, three-room shotgun house. As far as you could see, there were rows after rows of these broken down houses. All seven of the characters in the story had names that went along with their afflictions. One was Squint, who had a glass eye. His dad was an alcoholic. He had knocked Squint's eye out with a stick of stove wood during a drunken rage. Anytime a harsh word was spoken, he would stoop down and place his hands over his eyes.

It went without saying that Fat Bob had a glandular (thyroid) problem. Pogo had a withered leg that looked like a pogo stick. And then there were the Webb brothers. They both had an anger problem and fought all the time. Poor ol' Soup Bean was blessed with being the poorest soul of all. His dad had black lung disease and was dying. Last, but not least, was Wheezy. He had asthma so bad he would wheeze when he let his breath out.

Now the story goes that Wheezy had won all the marbles in a game, and a fight had broken out between the Webb boys. Mrs. Bean came out and ran all the whole bunch off because of all the racket. Wheezy gave all the marbles back so Squint would quit crying. They all went to the nearest saloon and promptly stole enough empty beer bottles out back to sell and get in to the picture show. The Webb brothers gave the bottles to Wheezy who then sold the bottles back to the bartender of the same saloon.

Well, they didn't get to see the whole movie due to the Webb brothers starting a fight. The whole bunch was tossed out of the show. The group then headed back toward home. Along the way, they passed the empty ice cream trucks. All the old and half-frozen ice cream had been thrown into the trash cans in the alley behind the truck garage.

Since Squint was the smallest, everyone grabbed his legs and lowered him into the barrel, and he would gather up as many of the ice cream cartons he could. He would "holler" when to bring him up.

Eating their fill, they wandered down to the Salvation Army Mission. This is where Brother Bob, Brother Ron and Sister Sally did their "work for the Lord." After the boys were told to be at church Sunday, they went next door for a batch of homemade cookies. Three "ladies of the night" had made cookies for the boys. These "ladies" would rock, sing to, and hug those seven little street urchins like the children they never had or had left somewhere along the way. In their own way, the ladies tried to save the boys' little hearts, and the Brothers and Sisters tried to save their souls. For the most part, they all did a pretty good job.

That day was the last time Wheezy got to see them again. He moved back to Hickman County in far western Kentucky.

"One minute and 32 seconds on the dot," said Pete with a smile. "Dang, that's a great story. Was it true?"

"Sure was," Lon said.

"How many stories do you have in that box, Lon?" asked Doc.

"Forty two," he said," but I call them Dreams.

"How come Dreams?"

"Well, when Daddy told them to me, it was bedtime. I don't know—they just seemed to sound far off and lacey—you know, like a dream."

"Now that you mention it, I can understand how that could happen," Doc said. "Let me see that marble."

Lon reached into the cheese box and brought out a cat-eye taw marble. "That's the one I used in *The Great Marble Shootout*." His voice sounded almost like a small child.

"Well, I'll see you later on in the week, Lon," Doc said. Hang in there, Pete."

"See you, Doc."

"As I went by the desk, the lady said, "I'll see you Thursday, Doc."

I muttered, "Okay, see you."

I was still thinking about Lon and the story. *Let's see, that must have happened 50 or 60 years ago Lon made it sound as if it was just last week. Every word was like it had been written down and memorized. How strange that anyone could tell a story that precise that had taken place so long ago.*

The next Thursday came around. I again found myself listening to a story. This one was about a little heifer calf named Brownie and a small boy named Wheezy. It seems that Wheezy entered his calf in the Fulton Fair. As he entered the ring, he soon saw his calf did not have all the credentials the other calves had. The other calves had big-named sires and dams. Needless to say, his calf wasn't even recognized by the judge.

Next, Wheezy entered his calf in the fair at Paducah. This time he had made a cardboard paper sign stating: Sire: Big Brownie; Dam: Diana; Calf: Li'l Brownie. Again, the same results from the judge.

Finally, he decided to enter her in the last fair of the year at Mayfield. This time he placed a small piece of paper, tied with a string, around the calf's neck. It just said "Li'l Brownie." There were only five calves in this category. As the 1st and 2nd winners were read out over the loud speaker, Wheezy turned his calf toward the gate. About that time, the awards for 3rd and 4th place were announced.

The old judge took the microphone and turned toward the crowd. He said, quite strongly, "But the best calf is the one I have seen two times before. In my opinion, the one named Li'l Brownie will make the best cow."

Now, Li'l Brownie didn't have the best credentials, but it goes to show how perseverance and pride will finally win out. The old judge strolled over and pinned 5th place on the little heifer calf.

When Lon finished his story, he pulled the white ribbon from the cheese box. He smiled like I assumed Wheezy did so many years ago in that sawdust-covered ground at the Purchase District Fair.

"That story was three minutes and 15 seconds," said Pete. You've got it down to a science, Lon."

In the course of the next year, I got to hear all the 42 stories in the box. I also got to see all the memorabilia that went along with each story. As time moved along, I found myself being drawn to the two old men's room more and more. I was soon memorizing each of the dreams. I was even able to tell them in the same time frame as Lon did.

There was a small note in the bottom of the cheese box. Lon wouldn't let me read it. He would only say, "In time, Doc, in time."

One night, Lon opened up and told us that when his boys were around 12 years old, they told him and his wife that they were tired of those old stories. They were also tired of the sugar cookies their mother had always baked for them. So, at that time, Lon had written the note that was in the box. He wrote it to himself so he could reflect on it when he reached a certain age in his life.

As the boys reached adulthood and married, they discarded Lon like they'd discarded the old stories and sugar cookies. They moved on and left Lon in the rest home to live out the final chapter of his life.

It had been two years into our friendship when I got a phone call from a social worker. She wanted me to see a young 14-year old boy named John. Needless to say, I was told if anything was done for him there would be no pay.

"Like the last time you called," I chuckled out loud.

"You got it, Doc," was her reply.

"Well, send him on over and I'll see what I can do."

"Oh, by the way, he won't let you look in his mouth." With that, she quickly hung up the phone.

When I opened the door at my office, there stood a kid who looked like he had been kicked around quite a bit. He reminded me of what the kids in *The Great Marble Shootout* story must have looked like. Sure enough, the boy wouldn't even let me look inside his mouth. For some unknown reason that escapes me even today, I asked if he would like to hear a story about *The Great Marble Shootout*. He nodded his head, so I briefly told him the story. After I had finished, I asked if I could look in his mouth now. He again nodded in agreement, so I finally got to finish his exam.

At his next appointment, I told him the story of *Li'l Brownie*. I finished all his work in that one appointment. He has been a regular patient of mine ever since. Many years later, I would learn why he allowed me to treat him.

When I told Lon about the boy and how I had told him his stories, Lon beamed with pride. I noticed that Lon was fumbling around in the box without looking, pulling out items and holding them. It was then I realized that Lon was going blind.

"Hey, Doc, take a look in my mouth on the left side. I've been having some pain in my jaw."

"Lon, I don't see anything wrong. Have you been having pain down in your left arm?"

"A little," he reluctantly said.

"Have you got your little pills that you put under your tongue?"

"It's around here somewhere," Lon replied.

"Well, find them. We better get this checked out tomorrow."

"Okay, Doc."

"Around six o-clock that evening, Pete called me and told me I needed to come by. "Doc, old Lon's passed."

By the time I got there, the staff had removed all of Lon's belongings. I sat down on the bed.

Pete said in a soft voice, "Got somethin' for you, Doc." He slid the old cheese box from under the pillow. "After you left this afternoon, Lon wrote something for you and put it in the box. He told me to give it to you if something happened to him. Now you're the official Dream Keeper. Doc, just 'cause Lon's gone, don't forget old Pete. Promise?"

"I won't forget, Pete, I won't."

After four years, Pete finally lost his battle with diabetes. Not long after Pete died, I retired from the job of caring for the nursing home folks. Late one night, I was looking through the old cheese box. I got a phone call from John (you remember, the 14-year old boy from a foster home).

John said, "Well, Doc, I've been accepted into dental school. I just wanted to thank you for all the help getting me in but, most of all, for telling me those stories when I was such a messed-up kid. There was something about those boys and that calf, about being so poor, that stuck with me. I just wanted you to know that someday I want to hear all the stories."

"That's great news, John, and yes, I'll be glad to share all 42 stories with you and the history that goes along with them."

Later that night, I got the old cheese box out again and opened it up. There with all the Dreams and items associated with each Dream was the note from Lon, tucked under the old Purchase District Fair ribbon. It read: Dear Doc, Fall is a time for preparation. It is very true that Mother Earth draws the very weak and very old near to her and coddles them. She explains to us about our *Long Journey* we are about to take. She whispers in our ear why the merciful cold winds prune the boughs to make room for the next generation. Wheezy.

All of a sudden, I realized that Lon was really Wheezy! I sat there for a very long time after reading the note. I wondered what I had learned during the years I spent with Lon. Finally, after writing several notes to myself, I came to this conclusion:

Oh what a shame that our rest homes are full of folks like Lon. They have been left there, like a receding river deposits driftwood on some uncharted sandbar. Left there to deteriorate and fade away with time.

If you ever visit one of these homes and you feel a tug on your shirt sleeve and hear these words—*Would you like a hear a Dream?*—take a little time and listen to the only possession they have left—their echoes from the past.

Poppy

Boo-Ray, Sweet Thing and Sidney

There Was a ring on my phone, and the caller was an old friend, Jim Brummel. His conversation started out something like this:

"Hey, would you be interested in going to South Dakota for pheasant hunting in October?"

"Heck, yeah. Who all's going?" I asked.

"Well, it will be Walter Lee, his son Joe, you and me, and a nut from Mississippi. By the way, he has rented a travel trailer for us to go up there in. We'll stay in a motel when we get there, but he has his heart set on bringing it along. Also, he's sort of a lady's man."

"Shoot, that's just great," I said and set the date to meet them in Clinton, Kentucky. We would leave for the trip from there.

All four of us had our hunting gear ready to go when the fellow drove up an hour late. I turned to Brummel and asked what the fellow's name was. He told me it was "Boo-Ray."

"Boo-Ray. What kind of name is that?"

"Well, it's his," Brummel said as the man stepped out of the travel trailer.

"Boo-Ray's the name, women's the game," he said and began shaking everyone's hand.

He was dressed in shiny clothes from the 50's with white patent shoes. His hair was dyed jet black and had on it about two tablespoons of the best Pennzoil motor oil money could buy. His sideburns were down to the angle of his jaw. He had possibly the biggest gold watch I had ever seen. Around his neck, suspended with a gold log chain, was a medallion that simply said *Big Boy*. He spoke with the most southern accent I had ever heard before or since. He reminded me of an accumulation of a very used car salesman, a southern politician, and a southern evangelist. However, it wasn't long before you could tell he was one of those colorful characters that come along every so often that you just can't keep from liking. I guess someone else thought so, too, because he had been married multiple times. The actual number of marriages was never really determined. He was now between wives and engagements, so anything goes, he told us.

As I entered the trailer, I couldn't help but notice all the hunting gear that was stacked in every nook and cranny. It was all borrowed, of course. I saw a new shot gun, down-filled pants, coats, and enough ammunition to start a civil war.

It was a hot October morning when we pulled out of Clinton. There was never a time on the way to South Dakota that Boo-Ray wasn't entertaining us with funny stories about illustrious past escapades. Some were real doozies but nothing like what was on the horizon.

We finally got to South Dakota and began checking into the motel. Boo-Ray asked the clerk where the best "water hole" was.

"The clerk said, "I don't know what you mean."

Boo-Ray got down real low and put his elbow on the desk and said, as slowly as I ever heard anyone speak in my life, "Where can ol' Boo-Ray go and boogie?"

The clerk said back, as slowly as he could talk, "The Dew Drop Inn Bar and Grill."

Boo-Ray politely thanked him and turned to me and said, "How about checking me in, Doc, while I go wet my whistle? Don't wait up. I'll catch up with y'all later." And, like a flash, old Boo-Ray was off to the races.

We all went to bed early that night. I'm a real light sleeper, so I couldn't go to sleep for all the snoring. I thought I would go to the camper and try to get some sleep there. The temperature was in the low 70's. A state record had been recorded for the high temperature. But the weather man said a winter storm was about to hit about 11:00 that night.

I climbed into the bunk that goes across and over the driver and passenger seats. I was totally hidden from view from anyone inside the camper. Covering up with blankets, I was soon asleep. I suddenly woke up to giggles and a honey-sounding voice—Boy-Ray's.

As two people came inside the camper, there were more giggles. I heard a man's voice, as sweet as chocolate from a candy factory, at the peak of his game. I could only make out a few words every now and then . . . "Oh, you sweet thing! Oh, sugar" . . .and so on. Finally, the words blended into one long string of honey, candy and syrup—more like a low hum.

The temperature had now dropped to the low 20's. That didn't seem to matter as clothes began to come off in every direction. This revealed possibly the largest mountain of flesh I had ever seen. There they were, naked as two blue-jays on the Fourth of July. They were full of enough anti-freeze to not care about the freezing cold.

Still not being detected, I was completely confused that anyone could believe what this man was saying. However, I guess Sweet Thing wasn't too choosy at this time in her life. It has always amazed me what alcohol will do for a man when he's 1,000 miles from home.

Things began to move at a more rapid pace now. Boo-Ray suddenly announced, "Nature call, Sweet Thing. I shall return."

He began to make his way to the rear of the trailer, to the very small room that housed the toilet. In his haste, he had forgotten that it was entirely filled with Brummel's and my hunting gear.

He said out loud, "That's no problem." He then went to the door and stepped out into the cold night air. By now, the temperature was down into the teens. The snow was being blown by a 40-mile-an-hour wind. There he was, naked and in full bloom, totally intoxicated, doing his business.

For some unknown reason, I took the blanket, placed it over my head and jumped to the trailer floor. Sweet Thing let out a scream from hell and began clutching for anything to cover up with. Alas, all her clothes were out of reach.

Now I must have looked like a combination of Darth Vader and Zorro, because all she could do was scream. Boo-Ray hollered back toward the trailer, "Don't worry, ol' Boo-Ray's coming right back."

With that announcement, I reached over and locked the door. I took off the blanket I had wrapped around me and placed my finger to my lips and softly said, "Shooh."

Boo-Ray started making his way to the door because everything inside the trailer had become very quiet. He started his humming again and he tried to open the door.

"Seems to be stuck. Say, Sweet Thing, could you help ol' Boo-Ray open the door?"

No response came. The next time, as he asked again, his words were a little more urgent. Finally, a scream came from that snow-covered parking lot, "Open the damn door!"

With that, I reached over and flipped the latch. The door flew open. Expecting to see Sweet Thing, he said, "Now that's more like it."

That's when Boo-Ray saw me. "Whoa, what are you doing here, Doc?"

Every inch of Sweet Thing's mountain of flesh was in full view. I don't know if it was me, the cold air, Sweet Thing's body, or a combination of all three, but old Boo-Ray's blooming appendage died right there on the spot. There weren't enough little blue pills in all of South Dakota to resurrect the effect—at least not that night.

As I headed toward the motel, Boo-Ray pleaded, "Not one word of this, especially to Brummel."

"Why sure, Boo-Ray, it's just our little secret," I said with a smile.

Making my way to the room, I could hardly find the key hole through all the tears from laughter. I just finished the story to all the other hunters when Boo-Ray came in. I've never seen four men laugh so hard in my life. I had only seen Walter Lee smile, but that night, he really cut loose.

The next morning, at the local greasy spoon, we were all looking at the breakfast menu. Up strolled Sweet Thing. Up to this time, only my brief description of Sweet Thing was all the other fellows knew. There was a "Wow, she's big." Then someone said, "Really big!"

Sweet Thing then said, "Hi, Boo-Ray," who was doing his best to hide behind the ever-shrinking menu.

"Hi," he said, barely speaking above a whisper.

That's when a new player stepped into view. Sweet Thing introduced everyone to Sidney. "It" had long black hair and was skinny as a rail, dressed in tight leather from top to bottom. It reached over the menu with a leather riding crop and gently pushed it from in front of Boo-Ray's pale face. It spoke in a deep voice, saying, "Heard you liked to party, Boo-Ray." The menu quickly went back to its previous position.

"Cat got your tongue, Big Boy? Well, we've got to go now, but look us up tonight if you want to play, if you know what I mean," Sweet Thing said.

"Yeah, look us up," said Sidney. "We hang out at the Dew Drop Inn Bar and Grill."

Walter Lee said to Boo-Ray, "When I was a boy, a circus came to Arlington on a train. They had a fat lady, billed as The Fattest Woman in the World. Let's see . . . that was around 1905 or 1096, I think."

"Thanks for the information. I'll keep it in mind." Then Boo-Ray rolled his eyes.

Silence hung over the crowd until a snicker came out of Brummel. It was quickly squashed by a hard stare from Boo-Ray.

We hunted that first day, getting our limits except Boo-Ray. He shot at 20 big pheasants, but at the end of the day, the score was pheasants 20 and Boo-Ray 0. When we got back to the motel, Boo-Ray perked up. He said, "You know, Sweet Thing had a right pretty face, don't you think?" Without even waiting for a reply, he then said, "That Sidney sort of intrigued me."

"Don't tell me you're going over to that bar tonight. Are you?"

"You know, Doc, you only go 'round once, and I think you ought to experience all kinds of different avenues. I'll see you in the morning at breakfast."

But breakfast never came, nor the next day, nor the next for Boo-Ray. It was finally time for the group to go home. All the gear and coolers containing the limits of pheasants were loaded into the motor home.

When Boo-Ray appeared, Sweet Thing was on one side and Sidney on the other. He had the look of a man just let out of a prison work camp. He was all hollow-eyed with blue whelps all over his body. They both pushed him into the motor home. Sidney whopped him on his butt with "its" riding crop. Boo-Ray let out a painful squall.

"Come back when you want to play some more," said Sidney.

Sweet Thing leaned over and gave him a kiss on his cheek and softly said, "You hung in there for a while, Boo-Ray." Then she waddled off.

Walter Lee leaned over the seat and spoke in the general vicinity of Boo-Ray, "I believe Sweet Thing had the circus lady beat. I'm pretty sure it was 1906." He then slid back into his seat and stared in the direction of Sweet Thing and Sidney.

"After three days, that's all you got to say, Walter Lee?"

"Well, you won. She looks to be at least 50-75 pounds bigger to me, but then, that was long ago. Let me study about it, and I'll get back to you."

"That's okay, I'll take your word," was Boo-Ray's reply.

"Doc, it's not one of Boo-Ray's finer hours."

"Oh, I don't know. Look at it this way. The winters are long and cold up here. I'm sure this has given them something to talk about all winter.

Some time passed after we all got home. I had another phone call from Brummel. I could hardly understand him for all the laughs every other word.

"Slow down, Brummel, and start over," I said.

"Have you heard the latest on Boo-Ray?"

"No, what?" I asked.

"Well, he had an older neighbor who needed some limbs cut so they wouldn't get in the way of the power lines" . . . laughter . . . "The old fellow had an old tractor with a bucket on the front" . . . laughter . . . "so he lifted Boo-Ray up to cut them with his power saw" . . . snicker . . . "Seems the old fellow hit the wrong lever and dumped Boo-Ray out. He was about 15 feet high."

"Did the power saw cut him up?"

"Naw"...snicker, snicker... "he was able to throw it far enough that it didn't cut him when it came down. But here's the bad thing"... snicker... "the fellow had a concrete driveway, and Boo-Ray broke about every bone in his body"... snicker... "He's now in a full body cast in the hospital. He's really feeling low and depressed. Why don't you give him a call. Maybe say something that might cheer him up."

I thought a minute after Brummel hung up and then called South Dakota to the Dew Drop Inn Bar and Grill and asked for Sweet Thing. I explained to her about ol' Boo-Ray's situation. I suggested we get a conference call so she, Sidney and I could all talk to Boo-Ray at the same time.

The phone rang in Boo-Ray's room. His nurse answered and held the phone so Boo-Ray could talk.

"Hi, Doc," came a low sickly-sounding voice.

"Hi Boo-Ray, this is Sweet Thing. Sidney and I are going to Mardi Gras. We'll stop by and see you on the way down."

About that time, there was a big "whop" of a riding crop. A low voice said, "I want to party, Boo-Ray."

"Doc, I'm looking you up as soon as I get out of this cast."
CLICK!

Poppy

Three Pats

It was a sunny, hot steamy day in July in the early 1970's. The smell of pollinating corn and honeysuckle lay heavy on the moisture-laden air.

The man looked down the road a ways. He noticed Sue Brummel coming out of the post office on the far side of the road. An old dog jumped down from a chair that was propped up against the shady wall in front of the office. Sue reached down and rubbed the dog's head.

The old dog, named Rudy, belonged to the storekeeper, Bob. He had been in so many dog fights over the years that he was blind in one eye, and one ear had been ripped off. He had been hit by a car and had lost the use of his back right leg.

Rudy hopped up in Bob's lap. Bob began to rub Rudy's head and to think about the small town of Oakton. He thought how much it had changed over the years since the GM&O Railway had taken up the railroad's ties and tracks. It had surely meant the death of Moscow, Berkley and Oakton.

The old grocery had been run by the storekeeper's parents. After their deaths, Bob had taken over its operation. Now, few came by and, like the rest of the town, it took on the look of being forgotten.

As Bob rocked to and fro, Shug King drove by on his way home from a poker game at Doc Mills in Mayfield. Shug hollered at Bob who laughed a quiet chuckle.

It wasn't long before a long, shiny new truck turned the curve and headed toward the small grocery. It slowed to a stop. Bob could see the outline of a soldier in the cab of the truck. He had on a beret and was the sharpest soldier he had ever seen.

The soldier spoke in a soft voice and asked, "Where would I find the home place of Lieutenant Bart?"

"Well, son," said Bob, "he's been missing in action now for about two years or so."

"Yes, I know," replied the young soldier.

"He lived up the road a piece, up past Hailwell Corner, on the bluff, but south of Taylor Walker's Fish Market. There's three or four roads and turns. You might have trouble finding it. It's getting close to dinner time. I'll just ride with you and show you where he lived."

"You're just going to leave your store unattended?"

"Shoot, most people just leave their money on the counter. Or they come back and pay later," Bob said with a chuckle. "Like a cold drink before we go?"

"That would be great," replied the young man.

Bob walked over to the icebox, which was half full of ice and water. He pulled out a small Coke. "They seem to just get colder in a bottle, don't you think?"

Taking a long drink, the soldier said, "That's the coldest and best Coke I've ever had."

"Told you," Bob said with a smile.

"Say, what's that great smell?"

"Well, that would be a combination of tassling corn, honeysuckle, and the Mississippi River," Bob said. "That smell creeps up from the bottom land just west of here about this time every day."

As the two drove along, the road suddenly turned from pavement to gravel. "Well, this is Hailwell Corner." Roads went in all directions. "Just go up the hill there, son."

That was all the directions the soldier needed. He said, "I think I could probably have made it alright."

Bob chuckled. "Yeah, but Mammy will have dinner ready. Maybe she'll have some squash fritters, my favorite," he said.

"Mammy?" asked the soldier.

"Yeah, that's what she goes by, and Pop is his name. That's what Lieutenant Bart called them so everyone just calls them Mammy and Pop."

"Tell me a little about them."

In a long, slow southern drawl, Bob said, "Pop worked at a place up river at Columbus as a welder. He could make about anything and fix anything that was fixable. Mammy stayed home and ran the little 50-or-so acre farm. The most noteworthy thing they did was to coach Lt. Bart."

"What do you mean?"

"Well, Bart was the best baseball player to ever come out of these parts, notably a third baseman. He got a scholarship to play baseball in college. He met and married a girl from Louisville. They had a son just before he was sent to Vietnam. Guess you know all about that, huh?"

The soldier just looked out of the window in the direction of the river and didn't respond.

"You know," added Bob, "Mammy and Pop worked with Bart as a young boy to help make him the best baseball player to ever come out of these parts. I guess you know he played third base."

Again, the soldier just stared out the window. "Go on," he said.

"He was so good he would play third base for each of the teams that were playing each other. On a Sunday when Berkley or Springhill would play Oakton, Bart would play for both teams. He got so good that Pop made a contraption that would throw grounders with all kinds of spin on the ball. He built it because by the time Bart was 12 years old, Pop wasn't able to hit a ball that Bart couldn't catch. You know what they called that crazy machine?"

"No, what?" asked the young soldier.

"A *Bouncing Betty*. It's the dangest thing you ever saw. Pop made it from scratch and painted it bright yellow. It could throw a ball 90 miles an hour and could make a grounder look like a squirrel scurrying on the ground. Pop would use that thing for hours upon hours until finally the boy would rarely miss a ball. Pop would tell him to keep his head down, charge the ball, and make a good throw. Finally, the boy would take his glove and tap his left shoulder three times. I think he named the little field behind his house *Three Pats Field*."

"Yeah, I heard Lt. Bart talk about that."

"You know something about what happened to the Lt., don't you?" asked Bob.

The soldier stared out the window and said nothing.

As they went up the bluff road, the soldier asked Bob how Lt. Bart had become such a good rifle shot.

"Well, when we get to Bart's home, you'll see the front and back yards are full of giant pecan trees. One of Bart's jobs was to keep the squirrels from eating all the pecans. He became one of the best shots I've ever seen."

"Yeah, I know all about how he could shoot. I could tell you quite a few stories myself," the soldier said with a small grin.

As they turned into the driveway that led to a huge old white farm house, the soldier asked, "Do you mind if I look at the river a minute by myself?"

"Sure," Bob replied.

The young man walked across the road and stood in silence for a moment or so. Suddenly he announced to Bob, "It's just like Lt. Bart said." He then walked up the lane toward the house.

The old farm house was totally in the shade. Huge old pecan trees were everywhere. In the backyard, he found Mammy and Pop sitting in a swing that hung from a big limb of a towering pecan tree.

Pop said in a surprised voice, "I didn't hear you all drive up."

Bob laughed and asked if it was about dinner time.

Mammy smiled and said, "I was just getting ready to set the table. Y'all like to eat a bite with us?"

"Sure," Bob said. "Here's a young fellow who wants to meet you all."

With that, the young soldier said his name and asked if he could talk to them about their missing son. He asked if they had heard from the War Department. They told him that they had been told their son was missing in action.

With that, the soldier began to tell a very unusual story about Bart. "I'm very sorry about this, but I felt you needed to know.

"About three years ago, your son posted the best score on the shooting range. I came in a distant third. We both were recruited by the CIA to be snipers. Hell, I never really knew just who we were working for. We were told that if something happened to us no one would have any knowledge about the situation. We were sent to Cambodia to kill the commanding officer—a Chinese general—of a Vietnamese training camp. A team of two snipers and two spotters were dropped off five miles from the camp. We completed our mission.

"A month later, they sent us back to eliminate the next commander at the same camp. It was early in the morning when the Chinese general came out on the porch with a hot cup of coffee. I could see the steam rising from the cup with my binoculars. Lt. Bart said, "Bet you a cold Coke that I can get him and the cup of coffee."

"I can remember smiling and saying, "You're on."

"With that, he put a round right through the general's cup and his head at the same time. It was the longest shot I think I have ever seen.

"That's when all hell broke loose. A patrol of Vietcong spotted us and dropped a few mortar rounds real close. My spotter was hit very bad. Lt. Bart ordered me and his spotter to leave and get back to the extraction zone. Lt. Bart took out most of the patrol, but a mortar round was dropped right on top of them. There was nothing left.

"He should have received the highest medal, but this is all you will receive."

He handed them the empty cartridge that had taken out the general.

"I was told to keep my mouth shut, but I came anyway to tell you. I'm so sorry. We wanted to stay with them, but being the kind of fellow Lt. Bart was, he ordered us to leave. He was the ranking officer so we had to follow orders. I saw it all with my scope. He fought bravely."

Tears streaming down their faces, Mammy and Pop thanked the young soldier. They both said they had known he was gone. They had both felt him leave at the same time.

As Bob and the soldier drove down the lane, the young man asked if they could stop for a minute. He walked to the edge of the bluff and asked, "Is that Wolf Island on the other side of the river?"

"Yes," said Bob.

"It's just like he said, one of the most beautiful places in the world. I'll come back someday," he said in a low voice.

"It will look the same. Not much changes around here," said Bob.

In the meantime, Lt. Bart's widow had met a man and was planning to marry him in a month or so. She called and asked Pop and Mammy if she could bring their grandson down from Louisville for him to stay with them for the rest of the summer. Pop and Mammy had only seen the boy on a few occasions. This would enable them to get acquainted and be able to tell the boy about his father.

He arrived with his mom on a Sunday morning. Both Mammy and Pop were caught off guard with how much he looked like Bart. He had blonde, coarse hair that looked like thatched wheat in the sun that stuck out in all directions from under a St. Louis baseball cap. His eyes were sparkling blue, and he had sun-tanned skin. He was a little larger than Bart was at that age. He would be 10 years old the upcoming week.

His mom said her goodbyes. He was left standing in the middle of nowhere.

"Come sit a spell and tell us about yourself," Mammy said.

"Wait a minute," Pop said, "where's your ball glove?"

"I don't have one, sir."

"What? No ball glove?"

"No, sir."

"Let the boy relax before you start all that ball stuff," Mammy said.

Ignoring Mammy, Pop plunged in. "Do you play any baseball?"

"Not yet," was the answer.

"Want to?"

"Yes, sir!"

Then it's settled. We're going to get a glove now."

"Can't we get it next week?" asked Mammy.

"No, now," Pop said.

Mammy rolled her eyes and said, "Okay, let's go."

So off to Union City to Wal-Mart they went.

"Pop, do you always drive this slow?"

"Now son, 40 miles an hour ain't that slow. Besides, we've got all day. I saw a glove like your dad's on sale the other day. Say, what's your nickname?"

"I don't have one."

"Well, we'll just have to come up with one."

"Everyone has called me Jr., after my dad, but I don't really like it."

"Being that you're the second Bart, how about we call you Deuce? That means a pair of the same kind."

"My very own nickname. Wow! No one has a name like that."

As they rumbled along in the old green truck, Mammy and Pop just smiled. After getting the glove, on the way back home, the boy asked, "Did my dad play a lot of ball?"

"Didn't your mom tell you much about your dad?"

Deuce said, "No, ma'am."

"Well, we have several weeks to fill you in on him."

"He was something special," added Pop. "Say, we've got six hours of daylight left. Let's break in the new glove. We've got to oil it down and mow the infield. Let's see . . . where are all those baseballs?"

"Wait a minute," said Mammy. "Hold your horses. The boy needs to eat a bite and rest up a little from his trip."

"Sorry," Pop said. "I guess I'm getting ahead of myself. I just feel like a lot of rust has been knocked off. You know . . . alive again!" A big grin came across his face.

While Mammy prepared a snack for the boy, Pop took him out to the ball field. It was located right behind the house. The boy looked up on a post and noticed a decaying board that said *Three Pats Ball Field*.

"What's that all about?" the boy asked.

Pop started to tell him about the sign, but he had to stop a second to control his emotions. After a little time and wiping away a tear, pretending that something was in his eye, he began to explain what the sign meant.

"When I coached your dad, I would tell him to do three things. First—to break down into a defensive stance and keep his eye on the ball. Second—charge the ball. Third—make a good throw. Finally, your dad would tap his shoulder three times, acknowledging those three rules. Thus, *Three Pats Ball Field*.

"Your dad put that sign up there when he was about your age." Looking off in the distance, Pop said, "I can still, to this day, see him doing that. Mammy was the first baseman. Your dad could throw the ball from third base as accurate as any kid I had ever seen."

Mammy came out of the house with her first baseman's glove and said, "Time to see what his weaknesses are."

"Okay," said Pop, grinning from ear to ear. "Go over to third base."

Deuce ran to where there was still a small bare spot where his dad once stood.

"Now, remember, break down, charge the ball, and make a good throw. I'll just hit you a very slow roller. No pressure. Okay?"

The boy nodded and tapped his shoulder three times, and the game was on. The ball dribbled down the third base line. The kid moved like a cat down the line, scooped up the ball, and made a perfect throw to first base. Mammy and Pop were so awestruck they couldn't say a word.

A few minutes passed, and Mammy finally said, "Let's eat a bite, then we'll show you the rest of the farm."

As the boy ran toward the house, Pop and Mammy looked at each other in utter amazement.

"Did you see him move down that line?"

"Yeah, and that throw had a lot of steam on that ball. I can't believe he could do that so effortless. Did you see him plant that back foot? Boy, this is going to be a great two months!" Pop was nearly beside himself with excitement.

When Mammy brought the platter of fried chicken, hot rolls, sliced tomatoes, gravy and a towering platter of squash fritters, the boy ate like he had never tasted food like that before. Mammy asked him what was his favorite food and the boy pointed to the now small platter of fritters.

With a mouthful, he asked, "Mammy, what are these?"

"Squash fritters. They were your dad's favorite," she said with her voice breaking. "Have you ever had any homemade ice cream?"

"No, ma'am."

"I've noticed what good manners you have, Deuce. Who's responsible for that good habit?"

"My mom said that was the way my dad talked, so I've tried to be like him."

"How did you learn to catch and throw a ball like you do?"

"Mom said dad used to throw a tennis ball up against a concrete wall when he was young. I did that all the time in Louisville. We had a tiny backyard, so that was all I could do."

"Would you like to see the wall where your dad threw his tennis ball?"

"Yes, sir!"

The old man and boy eased out the back door of the kitchen. The screen door slammed shut with a loud bang. Two squirrels ran up the side of a towering paper shell pecan tree.

"I wish Bart was here; he would make those tree rats pay."

The boy laughed out loud. "You tell them, Pop," he said with a grin.

Pop said, "Season doesn't come in for a week or so. We'll have them for breakfast next week with some of those fritters."

"Maybe," Mammy said laughing.

Suddenly, at the same time, she and Pop felt, after such a long time, the old place coming alive.

Pop began to show the boy the wall his dad used to learn to throw and catch. Pop asked if he would like to see Ol' Betty.

"I don't know what Betty is."

"Well, it was something I built for Bart when he was about a year older than you are. You see, it got to a point where I couldn't hit a ball hard enough to get past him. So, I made a gadget that would make him a better fielder."

"Okay, let's see the Betty," the boy said with excitement in his voice.

They approached the old barn where Betty was stored.

"I haven't looked at her for a long time now because it brings up some sad memories...not about her but about our loss of your dad."

"I know. It's my loss, too, Pop."

The old man patted the boy on the top of his head and said, "Grab the other end of the tarp and pull."

There she was, bright yellow. Even after all these years, not a rusty spot could be found.

"How does she work?" the boy asked.

"Well, it has a gas engine on her now, but I could convert her to electric." He took a second to design the results in his mind. "Heck, this is now. I'll fire her up and give you a demonstration."

After a little prodding, ol' Betty was running fine. "Let's see her throw a ball." And throw she did.

"Pop, did you see how that ball spun like a top? How fast will she throw?"

"About 90 miles an hour."

He had barely gotten it out when Deuce said, "Throw some more." So Pop obliged.

"Think I'll ever be able to catch a ball going that fast, spinning like that?"

"In a couple of weeks, you might be able to catch a few. Remember your dad was two or three years older than you are when I made Betty. I wouldn't be discouraged if you don't catch any the first time."

But Pop could see that look in the kid's eye, dying to give it a try anyway. His confidence was oozing from every pore.

"Cream's about ready to crank," came a call from the house. Pop and the boy headed back to the porch, chatting like two squirrels about everything known to man. The boy was so excited but not nearly as much as Pop. It was like old times.

"Do you like strawberry ice cream?"

"I never had any like this."

Mammy placed ice around the silver cylinder in the ice cream freezer. After sprinkling salt over the ice, she turned the chore of turning the handle over to Pop.

"Now, come here and let me show you some pictures of your dad, Pop and me."

Picture after picture was viewed with a small story going along with each one. Finally, the boy put his hand over the top of hers and said, "Nearly all the pictures and stories have something to do with baseball, don't they?"

"Now that you mention it, I guess they do. You see, Pop coached your dad for all those years so we could have a small part in his being the very best ball player to come out of these parts."

For the next few weeks, the boy and his granddad played ball and shot squirrels. You could almost see the boy growing with all the exercise, good food and fresh air. It was like he was expanding in all directions.

The time came around for the boy's mom to come pick him up and take him back to Louisville. The boy didn't want to go back. He balked when the time came for him to leave. He told his mother he didn't want to leave. This was where he wanted to be. To no avail, he was made to leave.

Not a word was spoken until they reached Kentucky Lake. The boy spoke softly but boldly, "Someday I will live and make my living at *Three Pats*."

The mother pulled over on the side of the road. She spoke to him with an urgent tone in her voice. "You don't want to go back there. There's nothing there for you. We have a swimming pool, golf course, and the best schools. You would have nothing to do. It's what I wanted to get away from."

The boy, staring out the window, said, "That's not home to me. Someday, *Three Pats* will be my home."

It was a long year for the boy, but summer finally came. He got to come back to *Three Pats*—the place he called home.

Each day, his granddad and grandmother would teach the boy how to shoot his dad's rifle and, of course, play baseball. The boy was very fast to learn. He soon became so good that one night at the supper table Pop told him that he thought he was probably one or two years head of his dad. The boy beamed with pride.

When the boy's mom came to pick him up, Pop took a long walk with her. He suggested that she get him on a Little League baseball team in Louisville. She realized her new husband was not very athletically inclined, so when she got home, she signed him up for the fall league.

Well, the rest is history. Because Deuce was so fundamentally sound, he made every All-Star team for four straight years. Travel baseball was just beginning at that time. He was soon picked up to play on a team that went all over the south. He played in 75 or 80 games a summer.

He made the high school team as a freshman. His senior year he was in an advanced baseball camp in Florida. A college scout saw him and called the University of Louisville baseball coach. He told the coach that there was a kid from Louisville that they had better sign before someone else picked him up. A week later, Deuce signed a letter of intent to play for the University of Louisville Cardinals.

Deuce called *Three Pats* that very night, excited about his chance to play college ball. "I owe it all to you both," he said with so much joy in his voice. "Are you coming to my high school graduation? Mom is throwing a big party for me at the Country Club."

"Well, I guess not," said Pop. "Maybe when you graduate from college."

"Say, Pop, do you still see Clay Gray much?"

"Yeah, why?"

"He said he would sell me the farm that joins *Three Pats* someday."

"Well, I wouldn't get my hopes too high, son. That's 75 acres, and land is going for as much as $200-300 an acre. Where would you ever get that kind of money?"

"Oh, it's a thought anyway," Deuce replied.

Deuce didn't get much playing time as a freshman but started at third base his sophomore, junior and senior years. He made All-Conference USA his senior year. He would call Pop and Mammy every chance he got. Finally, it was time for him to graduate.

"Remember your promise to come to my graduation. Are you coming?"

"We'll be there," promised Pop. "How about us bringing a chicken dinner?"

"That would be great," Deuce said. "I have a big surprise to tell you. What's Mammy going to bring to eat?"

Mammy grabbed the phone and said she was bringing fried chicken, squash fritters, grits casserole, butter beans and homemade rolls.

"By the way," asked Pop. "Can we bring Bob? He asks about you every time we go to the grocery store at Oakton."

"Sure," was the reply.

Deuce didn't tell them about the party at the Country Club his mom was planning for his graduation. Somehow he knew they would not fit into that world.

Mammy cooked half a day getting everything the boy liked. At 3:00 a.m., they picked up Bob at the store. It takes a long time to drive 318 miles at 40 miles an hour, but they made it in time for the ceremony. They met under a towering sycamore tree on the University of Louisville campus. They spread all the food on a tablecloth under the tree.

"Best food I've had since I was home last summer," Deuce said.

"Say, what's the big surprise?" Bob asked.

"Now, Bob, you weren't supposed to know," Pop said with a scowl on his face.

"That's okay, Bob," said Deuce. "Here, Pop, I want you to give this check to Clay Gray. I bought his place the other night on the phone. He's moving to Graves County."

"Where did you get that kind of money?"

"Well, here's the surprise. The money is my bonus money I got when I signed with the Cardinal Baseball Organization. I'll be in Memphis, playing with the Memphis Chicks."

The three old timers were at a loss for words.

"I've got a week or two off before I have to report in. I'm coming home next week. I've got some ideas I want to discuss with you all. You, too, Bob. Is that okay with you?"

"Why, sure, Deuce, any way we can help we'll be glad to oblige. What's the plan for the 75 acres, cattle or a row crop?"

"No, I'll explain everything next week. I've been doing a lot of homework on my project. I have talked to every baseball coach from Little League to Division I college coaches. They all say my idea sounds great and will do their part. They also agree there is not a whole lot of competition."

"I still can't guess what you're talking about," Pop said. "You've already made more money than Bob, Mammy or I have seen in a long time. It took Mammy and me 30 years to pay off our house and 50 acres. You're way ahead of us. Say, it's already four o'clock. We better be going home. It's a long way, you know, nearly 318 miles in old Betsy."

After saying their goodbyes, the three loaded up in the old green truck and headed her southwest. Deuce ran across the campus and watched the truck pull out onto the six lanes of traffic. The cars were zipping this way and that, as they slowly pulled out of sight. Deuce tapped his left shoulder three times like Pop and Mammy had taught him. This time, it had nothing to do with baseball.

Deuce played third base for the Memphis Chicks two seasons. In his third year, he was called to "The Show," as it is called. He played third base that year for the Cardinals, but they finished a dismal third place in their division.

A few months passed after Deuce's first season, and the front office said that they were planning on trading him out west, possibly to the Dodger organization. That was when Deuce said goodbye to organized baseball. He was blessed with his health. He had about 90 cents out of every dollar he had made. A great agent had taken care of his investments, and by everyone's count, he had become quite wealthy.

Deuce had a secret dream that had been hidden inside since he had been in high school. He had talked with every junior high and high school baseball coach all over the south. He had even talked with some in the north and west. He had shared his dream with all of them. When it was time, they promised to support him. Deuce was a very powerful persuader.

It was November 3rd, a cool fall afternoon, when Deuce drove up to Bob's grocery. Bob was sitting in his rocker, cracking hickory nuts. Deuce said, "Hey, old timer. Do you know the way to *Three Pats?*"

"Well, yeah, I do," said Bob, grinning. "What are you doing here? Thought you might be getting in shape for spring ball."

"Been there, done with that," Deuce replied. "How can I get to *Three Pats?*"

"Oh, you know, go down this road to Hailwell Corner, take the Bluff Road, and don't go to Taylor Walker's place. But hey, I was going up that way," he said with a chuckle. "It's gettin' about time for supper. Mammy may have some squash fritters."

"Jump in my car. I've got something to share with you, and I'll need some help from you, Bob. I never told you all of my plan three years ago."

"You got it," said Bob, his eyes twinkling with anticipation.

On the way, they talked about baseball and pro franchises. Deuce told Bob that it's a business and you are only a piece of the puzzle. "They give and they take away. I just left while I still had some principles."

As they neared the lane, Deuce stopped the car, got out, and looked over the river. He said to himself, "Seems like I've been around the world a thousand times and pulled a weight to get here. This time, I don't have to leave here. I'm home for good."

Of course, there was laughter and tears when he met his grandparents. After a while, Deuce said, in a serious tone, "There's something I want to run by the three of you."

"What's that, son?" Pop and Mammy asked.

"I've been thinking about this a long time. Now I have the money, time, knowledge and contacts."

"What are you talking about?" they asked.

"I want to coach."

A little disappointed, Pop asked, "Where? College? Pros?"

"Here," Deuce replied.

"Here?"

"Yeah."

Well, suddenly things got real quiet.

"Let me explain. When I listened to at least 1,000 coaches across the south, they all said they wished they had a place to send young and older kids...someplace they could have a concentrated effort to teach them the fundamentals of baseball. A place far away from telephones, music, and outside interferences. A place where baseball was revered. This is that place. I plan to take each kid and video him in practice and play the videos at night. I saw pros who had not had a sit-down, home-cooked meal in years. I heard every type of music from A to Z. The only music that will be played here at practice will be classical and semi-classical. I want the players to have three square meals a day—just like Mammy fixed for me when I came home for summer vacation. Each kid will clean his own plate, and one night a week will do K.P. Manners will be taught. Pop, I would like you to help me teach fundamentals and use Bouncing Betty at all times.

"Bob asked, "What can I do?"

"You supply all the food and do all the bookkeeping. Each of you will receive a good salary each week for all you do."

"Where are we going to put all these boys?" was Bob's next question.

"Pop and I are going to build a bunkhouse and showers. Remember, it's going to be in the warm months, so we don't have to worry about heating."

"Okay, son, we've kinda' mossed over here. I don't know if we can do all that. You know we're getting on up in years now."

"If you can't chin it, we'll add help."

Pop said in a slow drawl, "The question is, can you chin it—the expense and all?"

Deuce said, "No worry there, Pop. I can chin it okay. Remember it is going to make money, not lose."

"What are you planning on calling this idea you've got here, son?"

"Three Pats Baseball Camp," Deuce said. "That's the very first time I've said it out loud."

"Sounds good," Mammy said with a big smile. "Your dad would be so proud."

Pop was slow to respond at first, but now the questions flowed like a river. "When do we start? When do the first kids get here? I'm so excited I can hardly wait. What if they don't like the country?"

"What if they don't like my cooking?" Mammy chimed in.

"Relax, everyone. This is November. We've got until school's out in May. The first two months are already booked, and I haven't told anyone but Louisville coaches yet. But, getting back to the rules. The most important rule comes from my dad. Before each ball is hit to each player, he must pat his shoulder three times. Thus, *Three Pats* will live on. Someday, I want to go see some of these kids play. I don't want to be the only one to know about the *Three Pats*. We only have two ways to advertise here—word of mouth and *Three Pats*."

Pop and Deuce began the next morning designing and ordering materials. In one month, the dorm and showers were done. In another month, the bunks, painting and floors were finished. Next came the fields, three in all. They were laid out and seeded in February.

During this time, Mammy and Bob made up the menus and got extra dishes, pots and pans. They bought a microwave, a new stove and even a new cookbook. Bob painted and tuned up his old truck. He proudly added the sign on the side of each door: *Three Pats Baseball Camp*.

The month of March was dedicated to placing cameras for replay on all positions of the field. Finally, a new Betty was rolled out of the barn, with another the next month. At last, it was time for the first bunch of boys to arrive. There were a few final touches to add, like mowing the infield and putting down the chalk lines. Mammy had made all new linen napkins. All the recordings of the greatest classical music had been placed in the tape deck. Everything was ready.

The first school bus rolled into Oakton. The coach stopped and asked for directions. Old Bob told the boys to get out and to go over and get a Coke from the ice bucket. "It's the last you'll get for a week."

"Well, Coach, you go down this road 'til you reach Hailwell Corner, then head up the bluff a way. Don't go too far; you'll run into

Taylor Walker's place, Oh, it should be about dinner time anyway. I'll just ride with you all."

When they turned into *Three Pats*, it was is if they were in another time and place. As the boys got off the bus, Coach Deuce came out of the house and introduced everyone, including Bob. He told them about the rules. Then he told them to put all their things that weren't about baseball in a big clothes hamper. He promised that it would be on the bus the next Saturday morning.

One boy said, "These yokels don't have two dimes among them."

Bob overheard some of the boys talking about the goat ranch and wondering what they all were doing there. Bob just said, where only the boys could hear, "Boys, you're here to learn how to play infield from one of the best. You don't measure wealth if money is your yardstick. Now, go inside and wash up before you eat. Mind your manners around Mammy."

As soon as the boys started eating, Coach Deuce turned on the classical music. All of the boys looked up in total amazement. Not that they didn't like the music, but they couldn't believe anyone from here would even know about classical music.

Coach Deuce said, "You will hear this music when you play, eat and probably in your sleep. It has the perfect rhythm, and you will get the rhythm down pat. Now, pass the fritters."

"Fritters? What's that?" asked the boys.

"That big platter that's in front of you."

One kid named Freddy said, "You better get some. They are good!"

Mammy smiled and said to a young boy with big blue eyes and blonde hair, "Sit down here, son, and tell me about yourself." The boy reminded her of her lost son.

After dinner, Coach showed the boys the bunkhouse. He explained about some more rules, then turned on more classical music. Then he took them to the infields and explained how the cameras would be rolling the next morning. Their results would be used at night to point out the good, bad and ugly of their play during the day. This would take place after supper.

Each boy was responsible for washing his plate, and they would take turns helping Mammy wash the dishes and set the table for the next meal. This would be done while listening to classical music. *Yes sir* and *yes ma'am* would be expected throughout the week.

The first week went so fast and smooth that Mammy and Pop could not believe how quickly it all happened. As the boys began to file onto the bus to get their radios and games, they paid hardly any attention to them at all. The high school coach had stayed with the boys for that week. He could not believe the results—not only the baseball but the manners and overall attitudes of the boys.

The small, blonde-haired boy hugged Mammy good-bye and asked, "Could you send my mom your recipe for those fritters?"

"Tell your mom to write me, and I'll give her all my recipes," Mammy said with a big grin on her face.

As the boys pulled up to the grocery, the boy who had talked about the goat ranch walked up to Bob and said, "Sir, I'm sorry about the things I said. You were right. Dollars don't mean wealth. *Three Pats* is the richest place I've ever been."

Bob said, "A week of sweet tea and milk deserves a good cold Coke. Help yourselves over there in that old ice chest."

Just before the bus pulled out, another bus from Lexington drove up and asked the way to Three Pats Baseball Camp. Bob smiled and said, "You go up this road to Hailwell Corner and on up Bluff Road, just south of Taylor Walker's place. It's about dinner time, and if you will wait a minute or two, I'll ride with you."

The boys from Louisville started hollering at the boys from Lexington. "Wait 'til you meet Bouncing Betty. Don't eat all the fritters. Hope you like Beethoven's 5th." A big round of laughs came as the bus pulled out, headed toward Louisville, some 318 miles away.

"What was that all about?" asked the coach from Lexington.

"Oh, you'll find out soon enough," Bob said with a chuckle.

Week after week rolled by with nothing going wrong except a few cuts and bruises. Dr. C.J. at Clinton put in a few stitches throughout the summer. Soon, letters from other coaches came in requesting open dates for next year. Also, a great deal of praise came from coaches whose players had attended *Three Pats*. But the biggest stack of mail went to Mammy about the food and manners their boys had received.

One mom had gotten all the best classicals and couldn't believe the results she had seen. "He helped with the dishes every night. We would talk for hours on end about *Three Pats*, I guess you know he will be back."

"Of course," Mammy said to herself after reading all the letters addressed to her. With pen in hand, she wrote each and every one of the moms she had heard from. Recipes and advice about home cooking became her standard letter.

As that first fall rolled around, all the dates for the next year were filled, with a large backlog for coming seasons. Pop, Coach and Mammy enlarged the bunkhouse, added a new 'Betty' and made a new diamond, making four in all. Mammy was beginning to need some help, so Coach added a new staff member, Molly Muscovalley. Molly was a very bright and beautiful young girl. She had piercing blue eyes, and she had the appearance of coming from Ireland. She and Mammy bonded from the very beginning. Molly was the daughter Mammy never had.

After two more successful seasons, one day Coach Deuce said to Pop, "Here's a letter for you."

"For me?" Pop asked.

"Yep, just for you. It says on the front it's from Bunny Draffen. Bunny was the kid who was more interested in 'Betty' and the kind of grass on the infield than he was in actually playing ball."

"Well, I'll read it out loud," said Pop.

"Dear Pop, I got to play baseball my junior and senior year in high school. As you remember, I was only fair but still I enjoyed being on our high school team. What I'm writing about is, do you remember me being so interested in the playing field grass? Well, I'm a sophomore at Texas A&M, and my major is agriculture, especially growing a tough grass that I think might be used for infields. I have come into a great deal of money and have bought all of the equipment necessary to grow sod for baseball infields. Since you have some land, I was wondering if you and I and Coach—if he would want to—could go into business growing sod." The letter was signed Bunny.

"How about that?" Pop said. "I finally got a letter and maybe a new partner. What do you think, Coach?"

"Well, we've got a t least 200 acres now to grow all the sod you'll ever need. I think it would be a great thing. Wish I had thought about it."

That summer was about to change the whole complexion of *Three Pats*. From growing grass to keeping all three Betty's in shape, to manicuring the infields and keeping them in good shape, Pop was as busy and happy as he had ever been. Mammy and Molly had gotten new freezers and a new industrial cooking stove. Two times the number of kids to cook for, now *Three Pats* was in full swing.

A call from the Cardinal organization came to Coach Deuce. They wanted him to check on a kid that had been at *Three Pats* a couple of seasons ago. The boy, Drake Parker, was from Union City, Tennessee. He was an unusual kid who possessed many great qualities. But St. Louis was primarily interested in his glove and speed. He could also hit the off-speed stuff.

They sent two airline tickets. Coach asked Pop if he would like to go. Soon they were on their way to a jerk-water town in South Carolina. After seeing the kid, Coach called the front office of the Cardinals and said, "I think he's ready. He looked like a vacuum cleaner on third base. He hit two doubles, and he can fly around the base pads. Yeah, he's ready! We've contacted him, and he'll be in Pittsburg tonight."

Two days later, they were all listening to the Cardinals on a big old radio that sat in the corner of the parlor. The announcer said, "Well, I see that the third baseman and the manager are at it again. Maybe we'll get to see the new kid at third."

The argument escalated until the manager put the new kid in. There was one out, one on first base and one on second. The Cardinals held onto a one-run lead. With a crack of the bat, a ball was hit to third base. The kid laid full out toward the fence, speared the ball, and drug his foot across third base. Double play—Cards won!

After the game, the announcer said that the kid would be up in the press box to wrap up the postgame show. "Now sports fans, you are going to be in for a big treat. This kid is something else. A modern-day Dizzy Dean. Grammar ain't his specialty. He caught a late flight to Pittsburg the other night, and I got to spend some time with him. He's something special. Seems he owes a lot of credit to a coach by the name of Deuce and a place called *Three Pats*. But we remember him as a player who played third base in the minor leagues for a while. He had a bigger dream that seems to have come true."

Well, the kid came into the press box and took a seat. His voice sounded like an old banjo twanging off in the distance. He began to tell every dad in the country how they needed to get their kids to Coach Deuce and Three Pats Baseball Camp. He told how much he owed his success to the folks at *Three Pats*. Just before he got up to leave, he hollered into the microphone like it was long distance, "Mammy, fix me a big platter of those fritters when I come home."

"I told you," was all the announcer said.

In a couple of days, the phone was ringing off the hook. Parents were wanting their kids to come to *Three Pats*. Orders were coming in for infield sod. It was a mad house! *Three Pats* was on the map big time.

Pop, Bunny and Coach traveled around to high school and college campuses, delivering and taking orders for sod to be delivered in October. By December, Pop stated, "I just didn't know there was that much money in grass . . .this kind of grass, of course."

Coach turned to them and asked, "Do you all think we might make enough money to build a building that we could put an infield in?"

"Naw," Bunny said with a smile, "maybe three!"

The next year came and they had to have two shifts to accommodate all the kids that came. Pop and Bunny installed lights for all three fields so that everyone got more than enough playing time. It placed a big strain on Mammy and Molly, but they took it in stride. Old timer Bob made enough money to buy a used refrigerator truck to deliver the massive amounts of foods that were needed. Tired but very happy, the small crew at *Three Pats* had a great deal to be proud of.

There was a blonde, blue-eyed kid from Pine Ridge, Arkansas who just happened to sit next to Mammy one night at supper. He leaned over and asked her about when she and Pop were young, when did she start going with him.

"Well," said Mammy, "it was called sparking back in those days."

"I guess that's right," said the boy, " 'cause Miss Molly's and Coach Deuce's eyes are sparking when they look at each other."

Coach cleared his throat and said, "I need to check the bunkhouse."

Pop left to check on the Betty's. Molly suddenly had to leave to check on some rolls rising for dinner. As Mammy and the boys cleared the table, she could hardly keep from laughing. She looked toward the kitchen where Molly was still blushing. Mammy walked to the back screened porch and leaned her tired old forehead up against the screen door. She remembered a time when Pop was young. She glanced toward the small area where her son once stood. The spot was bare where the grass still didn't grow. It was like an old, old Kodachrome film that was etched in her mind.

The young man hollered to the boy, whose eyes were blue as the sky. His face was brown as a biscuit from the sun. His hair was so bleached that it looked like a shock of wheat sticking out from under an old St. Louis Cardinal baseball cap. "Now, get down and charge the ball and make a good throw," *said the young woman standing on first base.*

The young boy tapped his shoulder three times. "Burn her in here, Pop. I'll catch it."

Quickly, the film turned to slow motion, as the crack of the bat was heard. The boy sprang into a whirling blur. He scooped up the ball and made a perfect throw into the well-oiled first baseman's mitt belonging to the young mom.

"Good throw, son," *she said.*

All of a sudden, Mammy felt a hand touch her shoulder. It was Molly.

"Mammy, I wanted you to be the first to see it," Molly said with a shy grin. "Isn't it beautiful?" A shiny object caught Mammy's eye. It was a diamond ring. "Deuce gave it to me last night."

"Molly, I'm so proud for you and especially proud for us. We haven't had a wedding in our family for a long, long time. Hey, Pop, come look."

That was a very special night at *Three Pats*.

A couple of busy seasons came and went. Bob was sitting on the front porch of his grocery, making out food orders for the upcoming week. It was late April. A shiny truck pulled up and out stepped a soldier. He had so many ribbons on his chest you could hardly see his coat.

"Remember me, Bob?"

"My Lord, it's been nearly 30 years!"

"Twenty-eight, to be exact," the soldier replied. "I'm going to retire next month. I brought my son to sign up for ball camp. He's only 10 years old but shows real promise."

The boy wandered over to pat a box full of puppies many generations removed from Rudy. "Can I have one?" the boy asked.

"You can have as many as you want, son," Bob said.

"How about a Coke, Bob? I can still remember how cold that one was way back then."

"Over yonder in that ice box, son."

"Let's see if I can remember the way to Lt. Bart's house. You follow this road 'til it forks, go north but not too far or you'll run into some Walker's place."

"Close enough," said Bob. "It's about time for dinner. Mind if I tag along?"

"Jump in."

"Boy," said Bob, "put those pups down. They'll be here when we come back." Then Bob asked the boy's dad, "What's going on with you?"

"The Army has transferred me to a unit that builds and repairs everything employable. Then I'm running and ordering supplies for Fort Dix. It's not all that exciting but something that is necessary. I lost my wife to cancer two years ago. So the boy and I are going to start a new life somewhere."

"So, you can fix things and get supplies, huh?" Bob inquired.

"Pretty much. If I can see it, I can get an idea on how to make it work."

"Well, son, Pop and I are getting on up in years. I'm 80, and Pop is 86. We can show you the ropes, and I'm sure Coach Deuce will need some help, too."

"Who?" asked the colonel.

"The Lieutenant's boy. His name is Bart, Jr. Pop hung the nickname 'Deuce' on him when he was 10 years old, because he reminded him so much of his son Lt. Bart."

That year, more improvements were made at *Three Pats* than ever before. The colonel fit in like a glove. No wonder Lt. Bart thought so much of him. The boy...well, you guessed it...was well on his way to being a great ball player. He had been able to persuade his dad that those pups would miss each other, so they had taken the whole bunch.

It was late January. A light snow was on the ground. Coach asked Molly to take a walk with him to see the river. The snow crunched under their feet. The sky was brilliant with millions of stars. The moon was shining so bright there was no need for a flashlight as they walked toward the bluff.

Molly turned to Deuce and said, with some reservation in her voice, "Are you sure you're happy about coming back here? After all, you did give up the big city life."

He paused and looked out over the river and said, "Our team was flying from New York after playing the Mets in a three-game series. We were on a chartered flight to Texas. I walked up to the flight deck, and the pilot said we were over Kentucky. I asked him what part. He replied that we were over the far western part. He said he was in contact with the V.O.R. at Paducah. He pointed out the Mississippi River. I looked down and could see Middle Bar. I went back to my seat and had a funny feeling come over me. All I ever wanted was directly under me. That was when I knew the ball was about to stop rolling for me. I just wanted to come home. To answer your question, this is where I've wanted to be since I was 10 years old."

As he patted Molly's now-visible bulge, he asked, "What did Dr. C.J. say about the ultrasound?"

"Well, brace yourself," she said.

"Is it a girl?"

"Well," she said, "it has a dingaling."

"It's a boy!" He jumped, yelled and made snow angels in the snow.

"Well, so much for the girl," Molly said.

Coming to his senses, Deuce said, "There will be more, don't you think?"

"About that matter," Molly replied, "there were two dingalings."

"Twins?"

"Yes, a third baseman and a short stop!"

As they headed back to tell Pop and Mammy, they stopped to look at *Three Pats*.

"Just think," Deuce said, "a few years ago, there was just a bare spot where my dad once stood. Now, there's a whole complex. Some old pitching teammates called today and wanted to know if we could use them in the winter months and open up a pitching school. What do you think?"

Molly looked up at the sky and patted her belly. "I'm going to be out of the ballgame for awhile."

"How about next time working on a first baseman and maybe a catcher," Deuce said laughing as they walked home.

* * * * *

About *Three Pats*: If you traveled to western Kentucky and went to Hailwell Corner and on up the old Bluff Road, but stayed south of Taylor Walker's place, you won't find *Three Pats*. It doesn't really exist—only for me.

However, if you wanted to have an infield baseball camp, where the outside world was far away, you had the best food imaginable, baseball was played to the sound of classical music, and you wanted to meet the greatest folks in the world, "*Three Pats* is where it's at!"

Poppy

* * * * *

I had someone ask me about some of the characters that appeared in my stories. She asked if they were real or fiction. She commented that they always seemed so real. I told her they <u>were real</u> and were based on family and friends. She continued to question me about who they were. So, I decided to reveal the characters in this story.

Lt. Bart: My son Wes Mills, a great ballplayer and rifle shot.
Coach Deuce: My son Brad Mills, probably one of the best fundamental baseball coaches I've ever known.
Old Timer Bob: My dad, a very responsible man, who always seemed to appear about supper time.
Mammy and Molly: My wife played both parts—Molly, the blue-eyed 18 year-old beauty I married 53 years ago and Mammy, the very best mom I've ever known.
Bunny and Drake: Two of my all-time favorite kids who I was fortunate to see grow as players.
Kid from Arkansas: My son Cricket Mills, the softest set of hands I've ever coached.
Colonel: Jami Futrel, a boy from my past who passed away.
Pop: A man of many hats. I just saved him for me to know.

If you ever want the recipe for squash fritters, just write:

Mammy Mills
1310 Crowder Rd.
Mayfield, KY 42066

CPSIA information can be obtained at www.ICGtesting.com
229751LV00001BA/12/P